By Meredith Ann Pierce

THE DARKANGEL
(Volume I of the Darkangel Trilogy)

A GATHERING OF GARGOYLES
(Volume II of the Darkangel Trilogy)

THE WOMAN WHO LOVED REINDEER

THE WOMAN WHO LOVED REINDEER

THE WOMAN WHO LOVED REINDEER

Meredith Ann Pierce

The Atlantic Monthly Press

BOSTON   NEW YORK

FIRST EDITION

Library of Congress Cataloging-in-Publication Data

Pierce, Meredith Ann.
  The woman who loved reindeer.

  Summary: When her sister-in-law brings her a strange
golden baby to care for, a young girl, living in the
cold lands far to the north, is unaware that this
unusual child will help her fulfill her destiny as
leader of her people.
  [1. Fantasy] I. Title.
PZ7.P61453Wo 1985   [Fic]   85–47877
ISBN 0–87113–042–4

MV

Published simultaneously in Canada

With heartfelt thanks to Nancy Willard who,
at the Bread Loaf Writers' Conference (August 1984),
asked all the right questions

"J" is pronounced like the consonant "y." (Branja rhymes with Tanya.) "Sj" sounds almost like "sh" (*pisjlak* = PISH-lahk) and "tj" almost like "ch" (Tjaalsénji = chăl-SEN-yee).

Contents

THE WOMAN
WHO LOVED
REINDEER

I

Branja

CARIBOU was not yet thirteen summers when Branja brought to her the child. The sun, silver and haze-obscured, had nearly topped the sky. The moons, both in their first quarter, hung side by side above the far horizon. Caribou stood in the doorway of her *ntula,* gazing out over the mixed forest and tundra just beginning to lose color and come into fruit as brief summer hurried to its end.

She had known her fair-sister would come. The night before, she had dreamed a snow-bunting alighted on her windowsill with a sprig of bloodthorn in its bill. It had left the berries and flown away, crying its own name: *"branja! branja!"* This was always the way of it. Snow-birds were the messengers of the ancestors, and Caribou was a dreamer of dreams.

The figure of her brother's wife, lapped in traveling furs, emerged from the woods many paces from Caribou and struggled slowly toward her up the barren rise. She looked weighted with weariness.

It was two days' journey in summer from Branja's house to Caribou's, and although she was unwed, not yet in womanhood, Caribou lived alone in her father's house — because she could read things in flurries of falling snow, hear words in wind, knew all the old tales by heart, and sometimes dreamed. The villagers were afraid of her.

No one had offered to take her in when her father had died, last summer's end, though by custom she was a child still, barely woman-shaped. Not even Visjna, her brother — for he had been newly married then, to a woman outside the Tribe. His wife had not wanted to share their house with someone little more than a stranger.

Caribou watched as Branja struggled up the gentle slope. She was bearing two burdens, Caribou saw, one a bundle cradled in her arm, the other a deep sack dragging along the ground. Caribou did not go to her. Her dream had not told her what her sister-in-law would want.

As Branja staggered up to where Caribou stood, dropping her heavy sack upon the ground, Caribou realized that the bundle Branja cradled so clumsily was a child, just lately come into the world. One bone-and-leather fasten at the throat of Branja's *lanlan* had come undone, and Caribou glimpsed her fair-sister's smock, stained in two places from the milk in her breasts.

"Caribou," her brother's wife said, panting, not even bothering with the proper greetings, "you take this child."

She held the bundle out. Caribou looked at the tiny thing, golden-haired, fair-skinned, and flush-cheeked with cold, but sleeping peacefully. Her hands did not move from her sides.

"What child is this?"

"My child," said Branja. She was dark-haired like Caribou, but with the tan-shaded skin of the River-Valley People. Warily, Caribou eyed the other's jutting cheekbones and little eyes. They told her nothing. Her fair-sister held the bundle out still.

"Why do you and Visjna give it to me?" Caribou began.

"No." Branja shook her head, still breathless. "He does not give it. I give it."

Caribou frowned and was silent for a while. She did not understand. And then she felt a little thump of surprise as, all at once, she did. "It is not his child."

The realization unnerved her. She did not like Branja, but she would never have thought her unfaithful. Branja's face crumpled. Blinking, she struggled, her voice tight.

"It . . ." she said. "It is not his concern what I do with this child."

Caribou studied the infant's fair, well-fashioned features — so unlike her brother's lean, olive ones. She could not get over her astonishment.

"How old?" she managed.

"Midsummer," her brother's wife told her. "He was born two months ago."

While Visjna was away with the caribou at the calving grounds, thought Caribou acidly. Outrage was beginning to replace her numb surprise. Branja chewed her lip, picked at the edge of the fur wrapping the child. It sighed in sleep and did not wake.

"I have kept him as long as I could" — her voice

was low, a nervous whisper — "that he might be strong when I brought him to you."

She glanced about suddenly, as if fearing somehow to be overheard. Caribou, too, looked up. The vastness of the Wilderland surrounded them, empty — completely empty but for the two of them and the sleeping infant. Even so, Branja's voice hushed lower.

"But Visjna will be returning soon with the herd, and I cannot hide him any longer from the village — I cannot keep this child!" Desperation made her voice tremble.

Caribou tried to rein her own emotions in, to keep her voice steady and calm. "Did Visjna know you were with child when he went north this spring?"

Branja looked down, shook her head. "No. I do not know. I did not tell him." She looked at Caribou again, eyes bright, almost pleading. "If he guessed, I will tell him I lost the child."

Caribou stood silent. She was thinking of Visjna, defying their father and dismaying the village to marry this foreigner, this woman from outside the Tribe. *And you betrayed him,* thought Caribou, still looking at Branja. *Within a year you took a lover.* She could feel no pity either for Branja or the child.

"Why not tell him the child is his?" said Caribou quietly, full of contempt. "How could he know?"

The other shook her head. "He would know."

"He would not care." It was almost the truth. Caribou sighed. Visjna would care. Branja's betrayal would cut him to the bone — but it would make no difference in the end. Caribou closed her eyes, desperately wishing that Branja's faithlessness could matter.

She pictured Visjna disowning his wife, sending her back to the River-Valley People with her babe. She could not help the wish. With Branja gone, Visjna could leave the village and come back to the Wilder-land. *Back to me,* thought Caribou.

She opened her eyes and sighed again shortly. Hoping was useless. Visjna loved Branja. He would never cast her off. Caribou wished angrily that the other woman would go away.

"Show him the child," she told her. "He will forgive you. He must."

But Branja only dropped her voice again, her whisper growing frantic. "I am afraid."

Caribou drew back from her, surprised. "My brother will not harm you."

Her fair-sister's eyes implored her. "Not of Visjna," she said. She glanced at the golden infant in her arms. "Of the child's father."

"Who is the father?" said Caribou sharply.

The other hesitated. "A stranger," she said at last. "He . . . came through, passing southward, last fall."

A stranger. Caribou sighed, relieved. *And one long gone.* If it had been one of the village men, Visjna would have had to kill him. Then Caribou frowned as the last of Branja's words caught up with her.

"Passing *southward?*" she said. "Toward the Pole — in fall?"

That was strange. Only the wild herds, the rein-

deer, ran southward over the Burning Plain in winter.
No one knew why they went there, or how they
survived the cold. But always they returned in spring,
surging northward toward the warmer lands to calve.

"Was this stranger a lone one," asked Caribou, "a
tracker following the wild herds?"

Branja shook her head. "No. I . . . He did not say."

She drew breath, gazing at the child, her face con-
torted with indecision, or grief. Caribou waited impatiently. Branja seemed about to speak again, then
halted, swallowed, shook her head and would not
look at Caribou.

"Why are you afraid of him?" she asked.

"I fear for the child," the other murmured.

"What is the child to him?"

Branja's eyes flashed up. "He said that he would
take the child!"

Caribou tightened her lips. "Why give him to me
then?" she snapped. "Let the father have him if you
do not want him."

Her sister-in-law's green eyes welled up with tears.
Her full breasts heaved against the clasps of the too-
tight *lanlan*. "You do not . . . you do not understand.
This stranger — he is not as we are, Cari."

"*You* are not as we are, Branja," breathed Caribou.

Fury was choking her. She hated Branja — for
coming, for daring. For using the familiar form of
her name. Now that her father was gone, only Visjna
could do that. For trying to foist on her this bant-
ling, some stranger's, not even her brother's child.
The woman across from her bowed her head. The

infant in her arms kicked beneath the furs, slept on. Caribou's fury subsided.

"And how did this stranger know that you would bear a child?" she asked after a moment.

Branja shook her head, her eyes cast down. "I do not know. He said so afterward — just as he left me."

Caribou shrugged. "Perhaps he will not come back."

"No," cried Branja. Her eyes met Caribou's again. "I saw him. I saw him in the spring."

When the reindeer herds came back from the Pole, thought Caribou. Her jaw hurt from clenching it. Surely her fair-sister's lover must be a hunter, following the herds.

"Did you speak?" she asked her brother's wife.

The tears in Branja's eyes spilled over now. "No. He stood at a distance. But I saw his eyes." Her glance darted to the child, then back to Caribou. "He knew. And I knew he meant to return and take the child."

Caribou looked at her sister-in-law. Branja held the bundle out to her again.

"Here, Cari, you take this child — for Visjna's sake, not mine."

Caribou twitched. Once more Branja had called her Cari. Her blood was burning. *As if I could be cajoled into helping her. As if I owed her something — for Visjna's sake!* Anyone with eyes could see the child looked nothing like him. *So now I am to take the evidence off her hands and spare my brother the shame of being known a cuckold.* Caribou felt her heart close tight then, like a little fist.

"What would I do with a child?" she said, very quietly. She did not trust herself to say more.

"Raise it," cried Branja. "Care for it."

"For my brother's sake." Branja fell silent. Caribou let anger come into her voice now for the first time. "And how if your lover comes to me, demanding his child?"

Branja shook her head. "He will not come. He will not know I came here. I was careful. I told no one where I was going — I left no trail."

Caribou considered the other's heavy burdens, her staggering steps, her childhood spent among the Barge People of the River — not among the woodcrafters and trackers of the Wilds — and doubted she could have left no trail. Anyone could follow Branja. Caribou crossed her arms, her patience flayed.

"Why should I ruin myself for you?" she demanded at last. "How do I say to anyone who asks where the infant came from?"

Tears spilled again, streaking the Valley woman's cheeks. "Because you have nothing to lose. You live alone, far from any village."

Yes, alone, thought Caribou. The cold wind off the tundra breathed and sighed through her. Alone since her father had died. Alone since Branja had refused to allow Visjna to take her in. She glared at her fair-sister, but the other woman took no notice.

"No one cares if you have a child without a man," Branja wept. "Say the child is yours, or that you found it. Say that someone gave it to you — only do not say it came from me."

Caribou said nothing. There was nothing more to say. She uncrossed her arms, gazing off across the tundra, the woods, wondering what she must do to make Branja go away.

And the moment Caribou dropped her guard, her sister-in-law sprang, pressing the bundle to her. She closed her arms about the fur-wrapped load reflexively, to keep it from falling, and Branja hastily stepped back.

Caribou stared at the thing in her arms. Within its furs, still sleeping, the infant sighed and turned to her. Freeing one tiny fist from the folds, it closed its fingers about one of the long, dark braids falling over her breast.

"Here, Cari, you take this, too," Branja was saying, grasping at the sack she had set down upon first arriving. She twitched open the neck. "You see, I have brought you *pisjlak* — how do you say it? — provisions: caribou meat and snow hares, cheese, berries, sweet syrup, and *jaaro* stalks . . ."

She rummaged in the sack, half drawing out packets of this and that.

"I have ample *pisjlak* of my own," snapped Caribou, struggling to support the heavy child and free her braid. "More than I need. What I do *not* need is this child."

Branja jerked upright, dropping the sack. She backed away. "But these things will help you, help you with him."

"How could such things help me feed a child?" demanded Caribou. The infant's grasp upon her braid was like a hawk's. Still he slept. "A child needs milk. I have no goats or caribou —"

"There's *mmoli* . . ." Branja's words hardly carried now, but as she backed farther away they seemed to gain strength. "Oh, he will be no trouble. He is the perfect child. He sleeps and sleeps and never cries. He will be no burden."

Branja was now paces from the house, still edging backward and wringing her hands. Caribou wanted to follow — seize Branja and shake her — but the weight of the child was so awkward in her arms, she could only stand clutching it. She feared to move lest it slip from her. She had never held a child before.

"And these provisions," her brother's wife was saying. "They are a gift, a little peace-offering from me to you." A timid smile flitted now across her lips. "We are sisters-in-law, Cari. We should do such things for one another."

Caribou made to protest, scream, but all at once she found her throat was stopped. She had gotten better hold of the child now. His weight was still and comfortable in her arms, his warm breath light against her breast, and the tug of his tiny fists upon her braid almost . . . agreeable.

"What name does he have?" she managed at last.

Her brother's wife stood watching her. "No name."

For a moment, it seemed that Branja would say more, but suddenly she let her breath out as though she had been holding it. It was an outbreath of relief. Caribou realized that she had lifted the child to lay its little body against her breast.

Branja whirled, like a milch-goat suddenly untethered, and hurried away, almost running. Caribou stood mute, unable to move, watching until the other disappeared into the woods at the foot of the slope.

A sudden panic seized her. She could not believe she had been stupid enough to let Branja thrust this child into her care. Perhaps, perhaps if she ran, she could still catch her, force her to take back the child . . . But then she heard the infant sigh, just as Branja had done, and looking down she saw the little gold-haired creature gazing at her. The child had golden eyes.

A hot dart went through her, some feeling she had never felt before. He breathed again and closed his eyes, sighing in sleep. All at once her wildly beating heart grew still, the racing in her blood subsided. Absently, almost without realizing it, Caribou smiled. It had been a long time since she had smiled. She was no longer alone.

His tiny hand released her braid, and Caribou tucked the little arm back beneath the fur. Then she knelt and laid him gently beside the doorsill. Rising, she caught hold of the *pisjlak* sack and heaved it over the threshold, dragged it in to lean against the wall. Then she returned to the infant and, carefully lifting him, carried him into the house.

2

The Child

So Caribou took the golden-eyed child that had
no name into her hut. That evening, until dusk,
she left him beside the fire and ranged through the
woods, covering Branja's tracks against discovery —
she wanted no meddlesome villager trailing the Valley
woman to her door — and searching the brown,
crisping undergrowth for bitter, green-leafed *mmoli,*
that brings the milk to any woman's breast, even to
a grandmother aged half a hundred summers or a
young girl who has never known a man.

The milk came into Caribou's breasts in three days'
time. Until then she kept the child alive on caribou
butter, hare's blood, and a paste of powdered marrow
root, which the child laughed and smiled to suck.

Caribou tried to think of a name for him. At first
she tried calling him Goldeneye, but he would not
answer to it. Yet he laughed and cooed when she
called him "child," so "child" it was, with the golden
eyes, that slept and slept like some tiny sage, dreaming
wise little dreams.

Caribou fashioned for him three *bela* — sacks of
rabbit fur that could be layered one inside another —
for she had once seen a woman use such a garment

for her babe-in-arms. Then she set the child to sleep in a box beside the fire. He never cried, and when he woke, he smiled and took her long brown braids in his fists.

And sometimes as she dandled him, she found herself wondering, *What am I doing? What have I done, taking in this little creature that is no kith to me at all, only my fair-sister's child?* Had it been loneliness — only that — which had caused her sudden change of heart? The memory of that strange, hot dart when first she had seen the child's eyes came back to her. It troubled her sometimes.

But in truth he was so quiet that most days she almost forgot he was there, until her breasts grew full and she went to suckle him: at first light and mid-morning, noon, midafternoon and dusk, then again in the evening and just before bed. He never cried in the night for warmth or nourishment, sleeping in his box beside the fire while Caribou slept apart from him beneath her caribou skins.

Fleeting summer passed away. The autumnal equinox came and went, and the days grew briefer than the nights. Caribou dreamed of the return of the herders with their caribou from the summer calving grounds. Laying in the last of her winter stores, she dreamed of the wild deer returning as well, streaming south from the warm northern places where they summered. Soon they would pass Poleward in a great thundering train, beyond the Burning Plain, which only they knew how to cross.

It was the morning after her dream of the reindeer

that Caribou went to the hot spring in the high country. Hard frost was already on the ground. Soon, she knew, the heavy snows would begin to fall, shutting the passes and snowing everything under.

After that, it would be spring again before she might visit the pool. Caribou wanted to bathe there one last time before the snowfall, and because it would be a day's journey there and back, she took the child with her.

The water of the spring was warm and steamy, melting the crust of frost on the nearby ground. Caribou laid the child upon the banks, then stripped off her boots and leggings, her shirt and smock of skins, and swam naked in the hot mineral pool.

Leaning over the half-thawed bank, she freed the child from his *bela* and brought him, too, into the water, towing him along after her by his little white arms, flushed pink as a wolf's tongue now from the heat. He kicked and splashed in the steaming pool, under the pale far sun in the ice-chill air, grinning and gurgling. Then she dried him with a soft, scraped rabbitskin and laid him among his wrappings again.

At noon, Caribou emerged, dried herself, and dressed. She nursed the child and ate the small packet of pemmican she had brought, and left an offering of honeycake for the water-daimon. Then, setting the child on her hip, she wrapped her traveling cloak about them both and started down from the high country.

She had not been traveling more than an hour when she knew by the slope of the ground that she was nearing the narrow glacier-trough that rambled north-south between two rills of high country: the Reindeer's Path. She would have to descend and cross, then climb again through sloping woodlands to reach home.

A strange rushing sound met her ears as she drew near the Path. It seemed muffled at first, but grew louder the nearer she came to the slender valley. She could not think what it was at first and began to hurry, for the sky had clouded over and she feared suddenly some storm.

But when she emerged from the trees on the slope above the ravine, she saw what made the sound: not wind. She laughed at her own misgivings then, for below her thundered the reindeer, the vast wild herds sweeping like a river of living silver — all heads and antlers and backs, the tendons in their limbs snapping like willow flicks. They paced along, faster than human legs could run, southward toward the Pole.

The ground on which Caribou stood trembled. In her alarm a few moments past, she had completely forgotten her dream of the reindeer the night before. Gazing south, she glimpsed their rumbling train filling the narrow channel as far as she could see.

They must have been passing for hours, she realized, must have begun to come through just after she had crossed the valley that morning. Still smiling, she walked along the slope above the herd until she found a place where the hillside was not too steep, and sat down.

While she sat waiting for the herd to pass, she took

the child out from beneath her *lanlan* into the open air. The infant cried out with delight, his little mouth agape, laughing. Caribou laughed with him as he stretched his tiny hands out to the running deer as they hurtled by.

After a little, the rush began to thin, then to dwindle. When at length the last of the wild deer, even the stragglers, had passed, Caribou rose. Keeping the child still outside her cloak, she began descending toward the valley floor.

Halfway across the barren, uneven terrain of the narrow trough, she saw two figures on the far slope, one very tall and long of limb, dark-haired and olive-skinned: a man. The other, a woman in a bright-embroidered skirt of the River-Valley People, had the black hair and tan complexion of that tribe.

The man waved with his free arm — in his other hand he held a bow, the quiver slung from his hip — and Caribou recognized him then: her brother, Visjna. The woman beside him must be Branja. Caribou halted, apprehensive suddenly, feeling the weight of the child in her arms.

Just as she did so, before she could think what to do or say, she heard a sound: a long bawling like someone in great grief. It came from the north, the direction from which the reindeer had come. Caribou turned, but could see nothing beyond a rill in the floor of the valley where she was standing.

Before her on the slope she saw Visjna and his wife also turn, and she heard her brother give a shout. Her sister-in-law uttered a little scream and covered her mouth. The loud lowing sounded again, nearer this time.

Caribou felt the child on her hip wake with a start, his little body suddenly rigid against her. He gave a high, keening wail like no sound she had ever heard — it echoed the lower, louder cry that had wakened him — and began to struggle.

His tiny fists thrashed free of the swaddling clothes; his little legs kicked and churned inside the rabbit's-fur bundling. Caribou gripped him tighter, lifted him from her hip. Then her unease shivered into alarm, for all this time the child's small, round face was screwed into a curiously adult expression: not infant's squalling, but some deep-felt sorrow, his loud, piercing wail slitting the air.

Caribou shushed at him, tried the soft chattering of lips and tongue her father had used to quiet caribou calves — to no avail. The child wailed on and struggled even as Caribou bounced him gently, crooning to him, until his thrashing grew so vigorous she had to clutch him tight to keep from dropping him.

Without warning, his keening halted, so abruptly Caribou knew that nothing she had done could have stilled it. The child had fallen silent, half-turned in her hands, his eyes cast toward the rise in the middle of the gorge where they stood. Just then, Caribou heard Branja's second scream.

Suddenly she saw what it was that had caught the child's eye. On the crest of the rise, bright-lit, in sharp relief against the stark hills behind, stood a great reindeer stag of tawny gold. Taller he was than even the biggest stag she had ever seen. His rack of horns rose from his brow like a nest of golden arms and hands, webbed fingers wide-spread to the gray-bright sky.

He pawed the earth, stamped once with his great splay hoof, and the tendons clacked. The plumes of breath that shot from his nostrils made little clouds. His great, expressionless eyes as they studied the child in Caribou's arms were deep, pure gold.

The child reached out to him with a delighted cry, so much like one of recognition that Caribou was baffled. The great deer circled, pawing the earth again. His breath spurted and steamed.

The child laughed, and the reindeer started forward, then halted suddenly, stiff-legged. His eyes, as they settled on Caribou, grew dark and dangerous. She grasped the bundled infant tighter and stepped back. The golden stag lifted his head and belled — long, deep: a challenge.

Caribou backed away from him, toward the sloping hillside of the trough. From the corner of her eye, she saw her brother and his wife start down the slope toward her, Visjna running. The reindeer stared at Caribou, his head high, half turned.

The child began to struggle in her arms again, more violently than before. Caribou was hard pressed to keep her hold. Crying, he twisted toward the deer, opening his tiny hands, and reached out to him. The stag let go an answering cry, strangely mournful, and launched his great golden form toward them.

Caribou stumbled into a run. Her limbs felt light. Her breath came harsh and hard. Before her she saw her brother halt as he neared the bottom of the slope. His wife dashed past him.

Branja shouted something, interposing herself between Caribou and the charging deer, but the golden stag only dodged, lowering his horns, and feinted toward her. The Valley woman threw up her arms with a cry and fell back as the great deer sprang by.

Caribou lost her balance, her foot skidding on a stone. The child slipped, and Caribou clutched at him. She heard the dull smarting of reindeer hooves upon the frozen turf. Wailing, the child writhed in his padded *bela*. Caribou's foot slid again on the slick, icebound ground, and she lost her grip. The bundled child slipped free.

She lunged, trying to catch him. But before the child could touch the earth, before her hands could reach the child, a wall of gold passed before her, almost touching. The reindeer had dropped his head in passing, catching the infant in his nested horns.

Caribou heard a whistling, felt an arrow pass over her left shoulder, and saw it just miss the back ridge of the gold stag's lowered neck. Whirling, Caribou saw her brother reaching for another arrow from the quiver at his hip.

She spun again. The bending stag sprang up, snapping the antler-cradle high, out of her reach. Caribou cried out, her arms outstretched after the child, but the wild deer was already vaulting away over the frozen ground.

She heard screaming, and realized dazedly that it came from behind her: Branja. Caribou stood unmoving, her lips parted and the wind blowing into her mouth. Wind blew between the wide-spread fingers of her hands.

Visjna was running full tilt after the stag that held the child overhead, unharmed, in his horns. Her brother still clutched his longbow in one hand, and in the other, a long, slim arrow, double-barbed. His narrow quiver banged against his thigh.

Caribou felt her wrist grabbed suddenly, and jerked around to find herself facing Branja. The Valley woman clung to her, her wide green eyes beseeching, her words a breathless shriek.

"He came back, Cari," she panted. "Two nights ago, just as he said he would. Visjna was there. I had told him, told him everything, just the day before . . ."

Caribou stared at her sister-in-law. Words seemed to be falling from the other's mouth of their own accord.

"He came back . . ." Branja gasped.

"Turn me loose," hissed Caribou. "What are you talking of?"

"The father — the father of the child!" the Valley woman cried. "But he did not care, my husband, about the child. Cari, it was just as you said. Visjna told him to go away, stood in the doorway with his longbow. He told him the child was not with us, was far away where he would never find him . . ."

Sobs choked Branja. Caribou stared after her brother, the stag, and the child, and tried to drag her sleeve from Branja's grasp.

"We spoke; we discussed it," her fair-sister sobbed. "Visjna said we must bring the child and you to live with us. We were coming to find you! But the stag, the stag —"

Caribou tugged her sleeve harder. "Let me go, Branja," she said frantically. "So your lover returned — how does that matter now?"

But Branja was already speaking. "Oh, help me, Cari. Help me." The words ran and tumbled. Branja moaned, then cried aloud, "The stag! The golden stag . . . carrying off the child."

Caribou stared after the shrinking figures, now dwindled finger-small. She had no idea what Branja was trying to say to her. She cried out, "Let go!" and managed to break free at last. She sped away at a dead run.

Branja did not follow; Caribou heard her behind, crying and moaning. A long way ahead, she saw the great stag spring up one side of the trough and bolt away into the trees.

For an instant, her brother halted, fitted the arrow he held to the cord of his bow, and shot. He climbed on then, not even waiting to see whether the shaft found its mark. It fell short, striking the slope behind the reindeer's heels.

Caribou had nearly reached the slope herself now. Before her, the stag vanished into the trees, and a moment later, her brother as well. She struggled up the steep hillside, bent, catching at the frost-caked stub-grass for a better purchase. She reached the woods' edge.

And the last she heard of those she followed, above the harshness of her own breathing, above the soughing of wind and Branja's bitten-off cries, was the crashing of the golden reindeer and her brother through the brush, and also — could she be hearing right? — strangely, occasionally, cries from the child: no longer wails and screaming now, but laughing gurgles of delight.

3

The Golden Stag

CARIBOU plunged into the dark woods after her brother, the golden reindeer, and the child. She followed their trail of broken frost among the barren trees. But presently the trees grew so thick no frost had formed, and the ground itself was too hard to show any track.

The close-spaced boles threw vague shadows, and the day grew grayer as the clouds thickened overhead. She had long since lost all sound of those she pursued, and had no idea of where she was or how late the afternoon had grown. The black, wind-gnarled branches bent over her.

At last, she fell against a tree-trunk and leaned there panting; she did not know how long. When her breath came back, she staggered on. Her limbs felt thick and clumsy, heavy as iron. She struggled over the rough ground, half trotting when she could. A stitch had grown into her side, and her breasts felt tight because she had not suckled the child since noon. Thinking of him, she forced herself forward.

The trees gave out, turning to scrub. She came to a rocky place where the ground felt hot underfoot. The frost formed a thin crust, inches above the ground;

it broke beneath her step. Here and there plumes of steam rose through cracks in the earth.

She knew she must be nearing the Burning Plain, which her people also called the Land of Broken Snow. No one knew what lay beyond; only the reindeer passed over, every autumn at this time, seeking the Pole.

Then, all at once, the rocky country fell away before her in a graded cliff of steep stair-runs and blocks of stone. Caribou saw a vast plain lying below, faulted in places. Great expanses lay covered with unfrozen water, while fountains of pale steam spurted and gushed along the faults.

The earth, where she could see it through the frost, was in some parts grayish-brown, in others white as salt. There were pits of what seemed to be bubbling mud, and a line of dark, jagged peaks lay on the far horizon.

She heard rumbling then, and felt a trembling in the ground. Off to her left, the cliffside was fissured in a wide groove. From this trough, suddenly, issued a stream of white and gray, thundering, like a forest of deadwood buoyed along on a torrent.

Her dulled vision refused to focus for a moment, and then she realized with a start that it was the reindeer. They streamed from the glacier-canyon and fanned out over the Broken Plain, flying south. How had she outrun them? She could not guess, and was too tired to care.

As Caribou watched the galloping deer, small and far below her, the weariness in her welled into despair.

She thought of the golden stag, lost somewhere in that teeming tide, and the child bundled in his horns. Her breasts ached; her throat felt tense and sore. Her breath came in short, bitten gasps.

The child, the child. I have lost him — her mind nattered on without her conscious thought. She had never known she could feel such bitterness. Not since her father's death had she felt such a loss. *I never wanted him in the first place!* she tried to tell herself, clenching her teeth, but it did no good.

She wanted him now. In the short month since she had taken him in, she had grown so accustomed to the care and tending of him, to the weight of him in her arms, to his constant presence, that she could no longer imagine living without him.

Now he was gone — hopelessly lost. She would never find him, never touch or nurse him again. How long before he would slip from the golden reindeer's horns? He would be trampled to death beneath the drumming heels! Or what if he never fell — remained trapped in the antlers until he starved to death, or the cold killed him?

She could not bear to think of it, and yet she could not turn away. She scanned the surging torrent of silver until the afternoon darkened and the last fleet stragglers bolted from the trough. But not one speck of gold did she glimpse in all that time in all that river of gray.

As the vast herd of reindeer dwindled into the southern distance of the Plain, Caribou turned numbly from the rocks, back toward the woods. The autumn afternoon was very late, and she knew herself to be a half-day's walking journey from her *ntula,* at least.

She felt badly chilled from long standing, and she had no heavy, fur-stuffed *grimmul* to wrap around her against the cold, no flint for making fire, no food, no strength or spirit left, and she knew of no one living so near the Burning Plain with whom she might seek shelter.

Dazed, Caribou gazed at the sky. A thin, bitter breeze had sprung up. She spotted cloud-banks in the south and west. Dark, heavy, they looked as though they carried snow. Greatmoon hung very low over the hills, and Littlemoon was not yet rising. She quickened her pace as she reached the woods, chafing her arms.

Scanning about her, she called out her brother's name. But she saw no one, nothing but lifeless branches and trunks. No answer came. Her legs were aching. She called again, at intervals, until her voice was hoarse.

Caribou wandered through the close, barren trees. As dark clouds rolled overhead and Greatmoon slipped away, the afternoon grew grayer still. She skirted the edge of the warm, treeless ground she had passed before, still calling her brother's name.

"Visjna!"

Even in their fur-lined mitts, the hands she cupped to her mouth were numb. No sound replied. The soft, biting wind lifted her words away until, when she came across her brother's body not far from there, she was too tired even to weep. She halted dead. Her ribs seemed to fold in around her lungs so that she could hardly breathe, only gasp at the air: dry sobs. No tears would come.

Visjna lay prone, and must have been dead some hours, she guessed, for he was frozen to the ground. She could not budge the body to turn it over. Her eyes stung fiercely. They felt windburned, cold.

"Visjna," she tried to say, but her voice was gone. Her lips formed the words and made no sound. She knelt beside him for a long time then, simply staring.

Her brother's clothes were torn and scuffed across the back and shoulders — bloody there, as though he had been struck several times by something both heavy and sharp. She remembered the huge stag's great, splay hooves.

At last, when she could breathe again and felt her voice once more in her throat, Caribou laid her hands upon her brother's shoulders and sang the dead-song for him as the long, southern twilight began. Afterwards, she crossed her hands and laid them upon her own shoulders and sang again, for herself this time, for she knew she would be joining her brother's *wajn* very soon on its journey across the skybridge into the Land of Everlasting Night.

Visjna's parka was frozen to his body, but even if she could have cut it free, it was too stiff with blood and cold to give her any warmth. She managed to work his *ca'xat* out of its sheath at the side of his belt, and used the blade to slit the leather food-pouch that hung beside it.

Opening it, she found the little bag half full of travel fare, all frozen: pemmican, dried berries, nuts. She chipped at them with the *ca'xat,* working off a few slivers. But they were hard and tasteless as bits of bone. They chilled her teeth and gave her no nourishment.

So she spat them out and stared at her brother. A flash of desperation warmed her. He had no right to be dead! His flints and tinder would be in another pouch, sewn to his belt near the buckle, and there was no way she could get to them. *Wake up,* she wanted to tell him. *Wake up and help me . . .* The warmth faded. She was shuddering with cold. Nothing seemed to matter anymore. Surely she would soon be dead.

Then Caribou noticed a thing she had not seen before, as she eyed the blood frozen brown on her brother's parka: spatters of something else, little smears upon the body and the ground. Some liquid, now frozen dry — it was pale and it was bright, like purest gold.

Caribou stared at it, studied it, but could not figure out what it was. Turning, following the drops of gold with her eyes, she saw that they led off through the woods in the direction her brother lay facing, nearly the direction from which she had just come.

If she sat there any longer, she would freeze to death. Despite the leaden fatigue that filled her, her tearing hunger, and the bitter cold that clenched her bones, Caribou rose, stiffly, gritting her teeth against the rigor in her joints. She set out to follow the trail of gold.

The trail led her back to the clearing of tumbled rock and warm steam-vents, the place she had crossed going toward the cliffs and skirted coming back. The warmth of the earth rose through the soles of her boots. Her toes ached, burning at the gentle heat. She stared stupidly. She had forgotten the warmth of this place.

Pausing now, Caribou pulled off her gloves with her teeth and put her hands to the hard, barren earth to warm them. After a little while, rising, she followed the trail of gold to an outcropping of rock near the center of the clearing.

The tallest stones, reaching twice a woman's height, had thrust up from the earth in a rough circle, like a fort or crown. For the first time since she had left her brother's body, Caribou felt afraid. Her people called such rings of rocks trolls' hedges, for here the daimons of the earth gathered to smoke and play at dice.

She stared at the rocks, and knew that she should not go in. To enter a trolls' hedge, even by day, was dangerous, and to sleep in one, certainly death — so her father's tales had always said.

But she was very cold still, and night was drawing on, and it was into the trolls' hedge that the golden trail disappeared. She was dead anyway. So Caribou clambered up over the lower rocks and between two taller ones where the golden spatters led.

She glanced around nervously, but it looked like any other place: rocks and ground, and sky overhead. Taking another step, she came suddenly upon the stag, fallen forward on his knees, an arrow fletched with Visjna's colors buried in his ribs. He had been so close she had not noticed him.

His proud neck lay stretched forward, his throat and jaw resting on the ground, the cradle-like antlers balanced upon his brow — as though he had fallen to earth with the greatest care, to avoid spilling the burden he bore. No breath steamed from the reindeer's nostrils. His golden blood spattered the ground.

And there upon his rack rested the struggling bundle of the child, crying feebly, as though he had been doing so for hours and his strength was nearly gone. Caribou felt a pang of wild joy. She forgot all thought of trolls and dying, and ran to him, lifting him from the dead stag's horns. The ground was very much warmer here, within the rocks. She had stopped shivering. Steam-vents, closely spaced, were misting hot, humid air.

The child struggled in her arms, flushed, alive, his spent voice making more of a hiss than an angry scream. Kneeling, Caribou dandled him, cooed to him, laughing, unfastened her smock from the shoulder and gave him the breast.

The child ceased his crying and nursed eagerly. Caribou felt the pain in her breasts easing, and let him suckle as long as he liked. He closed his golden eyes at last, drifted sighing toward sleep. Caribou stroked and patted him upon her shoulder until he gave up his air, then laid him down upon the warm ground.

What was she to do? She refastened her smock, her elation dissolving. Her teeth were chattering again, for though the ground was warm, the air was fast chilling and the light was fading with the coming of night. Worriedly, she glanced around.

The enclosure of stones seemed completely natural. There was no disturbance of the ground or rocks to indicate that anyone had ever come there. She shivered and muttered a charm against the anger of the earth-daimons, then shoved the fear of them out of her mind and tried to think.

Caribou gazed at the fallen reindeer and ran her hands over his heavy winter coat. His body was warm still, unfrozen from the heat of the ground. Caribou took her brother's *ca'xat* and knelt beside the golden stag.

She put her shoulder to the body to shift it onto its side, then slipped the knife through the skin of the chest, drawing a long slit down the belly. The hide parted easily. Though heavier and much thicker-furred, it was as supple as rabbitskin. The pelt came away smoothly, bloodless from the fair white flesh.

She did not stop to wonder at it. Darkness was settling down. She pulled the hide from the carcass and swaddled it about her, fur-side in, laying the sleeping child upon her lap. Then she cut some of the flank meat from the fallen stag to quiet the tearing hunger in her belly.

The flesh was white as breast of ptarmigan, and tasted as though it had been basted in butter — though she knew it had had no heat sufficient to have cooked it, only the faint warmth of the ground, and the deer but lately dead. But this was a daimon place. Anything might happen here.

Presently, Caribou sensed her spirit returning. She felt strangely rested and well, immensely strong. Then, just before the dark was completely upon them, she cut the reindeer carcass into quarters and dragged each piece beyond the rocks and into the frozen woods near her brother's body, where the heated earth would not spoil the meat.

Returning to the child, she took off her travel clothing and spread it in layers upon the ground to be her mattress. Darkness had fallen. Littlemoon hung hidden behind the clouds. A light snow had begun to fall; she felt the feathery flakes touching her body, heard them hissing to steam when they touched the heated earth.

She unwrapped the child from his rabbitskin *bela* and gathered him into her arms. Lying down, she pulled the soft reindeer hide over them both, fur-side against the skin for warmth. No sound disturbed their sleep. No daimons troubled them.

That night, in dreams, she beheld no child, but a reindeer calf suckling all night at her breast.

4

Wisewoman

So Caribou brought the child into her home a second time, and afterward he no longer slept in the box beside the hearth, but with Caribou in her own bed beneath the golden reindeer pelt. As she had that first night, she turned it underside out, for the fur was clean and very soft. She loved its touch against her skin.

She rested all the next day, regaining her strength. The following morning, she strapped willow *binnakai* to her feet and returned over the fresh-fallen snow to the warm, barren place. She searched first for the trolls' hedge, to leave a thank-offering — but she could not find it, though she searched the better part of an hour and covered every pace of that bare, steaming stretch.

Her inability to find it left her baffled and ill at ease. Everything looked different in the snow. At last she gave up searching and left the loaf of tree-sugar on a flat, gray rock, saying a charm over it to draw the daimons. Then she returned to the woods where she had stowed the fallen stag, to build a drag-sled of branches and bring home as much of the carcass as she could carry in several trips.

The child came with her on the first of these, but he wept and fretted so when they came upon the stag, and would not be stilled all the long trek back, that afterward she left him in the hut.

Another thing puzzled her as well: she found that her brother's arrow, which had pierced the fallen reindeer's side, had turned itself all golden, like the blood. It felt heavy now and hard, and seemed to want to turn in her hand, pointing southward, in the direction the reindeer had run.

But what puzzled her most was that during all the time she was dragging the carcass back to her lodge, though she often heard the wild wolves crying like *waijen* in the hills all around, none ever came near the reindeer's body or harassed her in the slightest.

At the end of a week's time, when she had all the carcass of the wild deer safely stowed in the deep pit cut into the ground beside the house, covered with turf and weighted with stones, she returned at last to the woods to light a smoldering fire around her brother's body, to thaw the earth to which he lay frozen and cut him free.

She dragged him out onto open ground and burned him there upon a pyre of deadwood, with the proper laments and offerings. Then scoring her palms with a fox's tooth, she clapped them like a shaman and sang, "Let the skybridge be smooth; let it not be too narrow," because that was what her father had done when their mother had died, a long time ago.

This time the tears welled up, and Caribou let them

come. With Visjna gone, she was the last of her house: no aunts or cousins, no friends or kith. Of Branja she had found no trace. *I have only the child now,* she told herself. At last the fire died down to coals.

Of the ashes of that pyre and the fat of the fallen stag, Caribou made funeral soap, golden and smooth. She wondered whether her fair-sister, being ignorant of the ways of the hinterland, might have frozen to death that night in the snow.

Or, she reasoned doubtfully, as she washed death from the cabin with the tallow soap, perhaps the green-eyed woman had managed to make her way back to her own people. Caribou shrugged restlessly as she swabbed the close-grained wood with clear water, then dried it. She hoped so. She never wanted to see her brother's wife again.

Caribou made many things from the golden stag. The remainder of his fat she rendered into tallow, which formed many long, very thin candles, each of which burned longer than a whole lamp of oil. From the toes of his hooves, she fashioned cups for salt and condiments.

His bones she sawed and ground into buttons and counters and cuff-clasps and fishing weights, slivered into birks and needles, hollowed into candlesticks, fashioned into the handles of knives and the hafts of other tools.

But none of these would the child touch. Nor would he consent to be fed from the little hoof-bowls. He would not eat the meat of the golden stag when Caribou offered it to him finely ground, well mixed with fat and honey, though he easily took cheese and caribou butter or the flesh of hare and ptarmigan.

Indeed, the only gleanings of the wild deer the child would touch were the necklace of reindeer teeth Caribou now wore, which he handled and played with for long stretches; the golden pelt that was their blanket at night; and the golden stag's antlers, which she had lined with felt and furs to be the child's day-cradle beside the fire.

The child grew rapidly that winter, while Caribou fashioned things upon the hearth. He learned to creep and crawl about, well bundled, upon the reindeer hide on Caribou's bed or the furs on the floor. Gradually his infant's quips changed to more articulate babbling, though his cries could still sound uncannily like a reindeer lowing and he was a long time learning the sounds for speech.

His eyes never darkened to anything deeper than yellow gold, nor did his curls turn from their pure, pale blond. Caribou suckled him till he was fully two years old, that he might be well-fleshed and strong. And she called him Reindeer, in remembrance of the golden stag.

It was during the dark of that first, long winter season with the child that Caribou, eating of the reindeer's flesh and sleeping beneath his golden pelt, felt her dreams growing deeper, more vivid and prophetic. She had begun to bleed, in time with the moons, and so counted herself a woman now, no longer a girl.

One morning in early spring a drover stopped at her lodge to ask if she had seen his little herd of milch-caribou, which had started at the cries of wolves and fled away from him the evening before. Caribou told the astonished man that he would find the whole herd safe, grazing on a hillside above the falling stream on the other slope of the mountain, with a new calf among them, for she had seen it in a dream, drowsing by the hearth the night before.

Later, not ten days after the drover passed through, while Caribou was out hunting, she came upon a woman gathering red fool's cap in a basket. Without thinking, Caribou told her that adder's bark was much better for childbirth pangs than fool's cap, and that she would find some only a little farther on.

The woman, very taken aback, demanded, "How did you know I wanted this wort for childbirth pangs?"

Caribou blushed, realizing what she had done. "I dreamed it," she stammered, and glimpsed the woman making the sign against evil behind the basket.

"You're Visjna's sister, aren't you?" the woman said nervously. She was holding the basket in front of her as if to keep Caribou away. "The one who sees things."

Caribou felt her blush deepening. Her hands on the bow shaft tightened. So the village people were still afraid of her. She nodded, saying nothing. The village woman was edging away.

"No one's seen Visjna, nor his wife — that Valley woman — since the fall," she started.

"Visjna's dead." Caribou made herself say it. The words came out harsh. She was not used to talking to strangers, and if she said much of Visjna she was afraid she might weep. "One of the wild deer killed him. I found him and burned him." She blinked hard and bit her lip. "I didn't find Branja."

The village woman came no nearer, but her stance seemed to relax a little. Her tone, when she spoke, had softened. "You're . . . you're younger than I thought," she said at last. "I've a girl about your age."

Caribou's eyes flashed up. "I'm a woman," she hissed. The other flinched but did not run. She fingered the basket uncertainly. She seemed at a loss. Caribou shouldered her bow and started upslope past her. "Do your gathering and get home quickly," she added, more softly now. "Your sister will be in labor before her time — before moonrise."

The woman was staring at her again. "Visjna's sister —" she began.

Caribou halted. "My name is Caribou," she said.

The other nodded. "My thanks for your help, Visj — Caribou." She sounded sincere.

Caribou felt something tugging at the corner of her mouth. In a moment, she realized, surprised, that it was a smile. The village woman managed a smile in return. Caribou turned and continued through the trees. Oddly, her heart felt lighter than it had in days.

There had been no fear on the other's face just then, at the last, only curiosity. *Or pity?* Caribou sighed. The villagers were strange to her, their lives as far away from hers as the unseen moons. She despaired of ever touching them. She sighed again. The day was late, and she had not found so much as a ptarmigan yet. She shoved the thought of the woman with the basket from her mind and hurried on in search of game.

After that, people sometimes sought Caribou out to ask advice — only a few from the nearby villages at first, but gradually more and more, until she began to earn for herself the name of wisewoman. In the beginning it was difficult, meeting so many strangers and deciding what they should do, but after a time she caught the knack of it.

When they came, she gave them food and drink, then sat upon the doorstep of her *ntula,* with the child beside her and the golden arrow on her lap, listening to their concerns. After much thinking and running of her fingers along the smooth yellow shaft, she would tell them what they wanted to know: why it was their nannies would not bring forth live kids, or where lost articles were to be found, or which would be the better man to wed.

They went away, back to their farms and villages, thanking her with smiles and gifts. Sometimes they came a second time, either for themselves or bringing someone else who needed help. Always those who

came again said Caribou's advice on the other matter
had been good and that things had been as she had
said.

Sometimes it was things she remembered seeing in
her dreams, and other times it was her own weighing
of their words that determined what she told them;
but always, when they went away, they seemed satisfied. Caribou found her heart opening out a little at
last, to see people grateful to her and not so much
afraid anymore.

She felt happier, less of an outcast from her Tribe.
She had been alone a long time, with only the golden
child to comfort her. Now, before two or three years
had gone by, not a fortnight passed without some
traveler footing the new-worn path to her lonely hut
to ask the wisewoman's advice.

Only one thing troubled her, and that was Reindeer. While still she suckled him, he usually sat on
her lap when she answered those who came, and later,
when he was older, on the step beside her, listening
to her and watching the others with his great, still,
luminous eyes.

Later, when they had gone, he would question her
about them, who they were and where they came
from, how they lived, why they needed her advice
and why she had told them what she had. The strangers
fascinated him.

"They are not like us, are they, Cari?" he asked her
once, a question that puzzled her.

"No," she answered, "for they live together in villages, or on farms outside of villages, and we live here in the Wilderland, alone."

She answered his other questions as best she could. Although he was brighter and quicker than other children she saw, even children older than he, he did not always seem to understand.

"You told that man who came to you this morning to marry the woman who loved him," the child said to her one afternoon, "and forget the one who would cause him sorrow."

Sitting upon her lap beside the cutting table outside, he was using a broad-bladed chop with laborious care to dice the red rushes for their dinner. Caribou guided his small, square hands.

"Why?" Reindeer asked her. "Why did you say those things to him?"

Caribou laughed, squeezing his cool fingers. "Did that not seem sound advice to you?"

The sun was bright. The metal blade went chop, and chop. "What's love?" the child said. "What's sorrow?"

Caribou frowned, puzzled. She did not know what to make of the questions. "Love is . . ." she said. "Love is what I feel for you — and you for me, I hope."

Reindeer had laid the square blade down. All the rushes were cut and oozing clear, sweet juice. His face was blank. "I don't understand."

Caribou pursed her lips, perturbed, and swept the

rushes into a clay pot to be steamed. She found his questions very odd. How could a person, even a child, not know what love was?

"I take care of you," she began, "because I love you . . ."

The boy on her lap shifted, turning to look at her. "I don't take care of *you*."

Caribou sighed. "No, but you love me just the same — because I love you."

Reindeer did not say anything. Caribou laid the pot of rushes down and drew breath to try again, but the boy spoke first, getting down from her lap. His golden eyes looked deep into hers.

"And sorrow?"

Caribou despaired. "Sorrow is," she began. "It is what you feel if someone hurts you, or if someone you love is hurt — or is gone from you." She felt ridiculous trying to put it into words. No one had ever explained such things to her. She simply knew.

Reindeer nodded then, very thoughtfully — though she had an eerie feeling that even now he had no inkling what she meant. The people from the villages called her wisewoman because she could see things in dreams. But she never dreamed about Reindeer. He was a mystery to her.

5

Reindeer

TIME PASSED. Reindeer grew a year older, and Caribou came no closer to understanding him. Sometimes she saw people who came to her murmuring behind their hands and looking at him. They whispered that he was odd, with his yellow hair and fair, white skin, though to her face they said he was a fine boy, strapping and strong, very comely to look at.

And Caribou, who knew nothing of beauty that was not in the lay of the land, or in livestock or household things, gazed at the fine-planed features of her growing boy, and was not sure. But when they asked who he was, she answered always, "My brother's child, not mine."

She had never thought of him as hers somehow, even after so long. No tie of blood bound them, and the older he grew, the less he seemed like her or the others of her Tribe. He was a strange child, very solemn now, who neither laughed nor cried anymore, and rarely spoke.

He sat beside her in the evenings on the hearthstone, listening to some tale she might be telling, half to

herself and half to him, and playing with the necklace
of reindeer teeth upon her breast.

Tales of *iff*s and *ont*s and other kinds of daimons —
trolls that played at dice, and cave-boggles, sea-maidens
with gray-green hair, and halflings that could change
their skins. Tales of ghostly *waijen,* the ancestors, who
lived beyond the skybridge in the Land of Everlasting
Night, and could be seen dancing in the southern sky
on winter evenings in shimmering trains of red and
green.

Reindeer never tired of them — all the tales Caribou's father had told her before his death. She hardly
missed him now that Reindeer had come. One evening he turned to her as they sat upon the hearth. He
was very small still, but seemed far older than his
age.

He asked her, "Cari, what is a *trangl?*"

Caribou looked up from the basket she was mending and frowned. She knew the word, but could not
remember what it meant. "Why do you ask?" she
said. "Where did you hear of it?"

The boy replied, "I overheard the people who came
to see you today using it. Do they lie with men?"

"What?"

"The *traangol.* Do they lie with men? The people
were saying one of the men of their village had been
charmed by one." Reindeer shifted upon the hearth.
"What is one? Is it a daimon?"

Caribou nodded and picked up her basket again.
She remembered now. "Yes. A kind of daimon that
can walk in human shape."

Reindeer watched her. "Why have you told me no tales of them?" he asked.

"I don't know any," Caribou replied, deftly teasing out the broken strip of basket-bark from the others. "My brother Visjna would have known." She sighed. Even four years after, her breast still tightened at the thought of Visjna. "He tended my father's caribou and sometimes spoke to *kaaluwati,* who track the wild deer and tell tales of such things — but he is dead."

She shook her head, trying to banish the painful memory, and began paring a new strip of bark very carefully. Just then a log in the fire burst, in a rain of sparks, and the knife slipped in her hand. A line of blood welled up from her thumb, and Caribou dropped blade and basket with a curse.

"What's that?" said Reindeer suddenly, staring at her hand. "Cari, what's that?"

Caribou bit down on her thumb to make the bleeding stop, and glanced at him. "It's blood," she said, puzzled, reaching to show him. "Don't you know?"

He took her hand on his lap and gazed at the dark trickle there, intrigued.

"It's red," he said.

"Of course." She took her hand back, went to get a clean strip of woven cloth. "Like animals' blood. Like the hares I bring home." She wrapped the linen around her thumb. "What color did you think it would be?"

Reindeer never took his eyes from her, but scratched the back of his neck meditatively. Caribou sat back down on the hearth.

"Will I ever bleed like that, Cari?"

He asked it so solemnly that Caribou laughed.

"Not if you don't cut yourself," she replied, and picked the basket up again.

For a moment, she thought he might say more, but he only nodded. Already he was turning back toward the fire — indeed, sometimes he sat, hands on lap, and stared into the coals so long and so still that Caribou was sure he had fallen asleep with his eyes open. But whenever she spoke, he turned and answered her without starting.

He was restless in spring when the reindeer were running, and seemed to know to the moment when they had returned. Caribou often found him, at the end of the day in the twilight, gazing off toward the chilly southlands until the wild herds had passed north to the warmer calving grounds. Then he gazed northward for the rest of the season.

He was like the golden arrow, she thought, which, no matter how she laid it upon the shelf above the hearth, always seemed to have turned itself northward after a little, in spring. It was the same in winter, though then the arrow pointed Poleward, and Reindeer too gazed southward again, to where the reindeer had passed beyond the Burning Plain.

And sometimes at day's end, when she saw him sitting at hearthside or staring off into the twilight, wholly absorbed, oblivious to her, more still than any creature she had ever seen, she found herself marveling, lost in a dream that he was no human child at all, but some strange other thing that had no human heart.

Yet, for all his strangeness, he was her only joy. Caribou could not say how, before he came, she had borne the solitude. He was her companion in the day-chores of the lodge — building and mending and splitting wood for the fire — and he shared the reindeer coverlet with her at night.

As soon as he was old enough, he accompanied her wood-gathering, or berry-picking, or checking her snares. And before much longer, she could send him out by himself on one errand while she herself attended to another.

There was no greater happiness for her than to await his homecoming of an evening, or to come home to him at dusk on those days when it had been her turn to check the traps, to find him waiting on the doorsill and have him come out to meet her, put his arms about her waist, and gaze at her with his great gold eyes and ask her solemnly what luck the traps had had that day.

Then one day when Reindeer was nearly five summers old, something happened that troubled Caribou more than she could say. It was springtime, the ice of winter gone and the rush of melting snow now past. Caribou had taken him with her fishing for salmon in the quiet stream that wended past the rise on which their *ntula* stood.

She had been sitting a long time on the stony bank

with her fishing line wrapped around a shuttle that lay in her lap. Reindeer had wandered away, but she felt no alarm. He was a remarkably safe child, and seemed never to lose or injure himself. She had never seen him bruised or scraped. He would be back in his own time, when it suited him. Dozing, she dreamed a fish stole the bait from her line.

Something startled her awake, and she sat very still, listening, but heard nothing. Then after a moment, she realized that in the water before her, beside her own reflection, was the image of a reindeer calf.

She made no sound, not wanting to frighten it, and wondered what calf this could be, so well grown so early in the season, and so far south of the calving grounds — unless it were the calf of someone's milch-caribou, wandered off from its dam.

The calf was watching her and not its own reflection. She did not move or turn, was just preparing to cluck softly, in hopes of coaxing it close enough to catch, when Reindeer's voice sounded, so near it made her jump.

"There's a fish nibbling your line, Cari."

Caribou caught in her breath, started to her feet and whirled. Reindeer stood upon the bank and no caribou calf.

"Where is it?" she stammered. "Did you chase it away?"

"Chase what," the boy replied, "the fish? No, it's still on the line."

"The calf," cried Caribou, glancing into the woods behind him, trying to spot it.

"What calf?" said Reindeer. "You've dropped your framework, and the fish is pulling it into the water."

Caribou gave an exasperated sigh, turned back to the stream to retrieve the line — and halted dead. Beside her own reflection in the water still stood that of the reindeer calf. She whirled. Nothing stood there but Reindeer, her boy.

Reindeer moved one hand slightly, scratching his wrist. A gasp caught in Caribou's throat as she gazed at the image of the calf in the water, scratching one foreleg with its hoof. She turned and stared at Reindeer.

"What is it?" he murmured, frowning, then gestured beyond her. "You're going to lose it, the fishing line."

Caribou backed away from him on the bank, bent down to fish the framework from the water without looking at it. The stream was icy on her hand. Reindeer still looked at her; he had taken no notice yet of his own reflection.

"Get . . . get back from the water," she stammered. She must not let him see. The water held something unearthly, so strange she could not understand it. Some trick of the water-daimon? Hurriedly, she searched her memory, but could remember no tale that spoke of such a thing. "You're standing too near," she told Reindeer. "You might fall."

The boy retreated a few paces from the bank. Caribou got hold of the fishing line and straightened, pulling too hard. She felt the fish slip from the hook.

"What is it?" said Reindeer, coming a pace closer to her. "Cari, what's frightened you?"

"Nothing," she said, coming toward him lest he draw near enough to the water again to see himself. She wound the draggled fishline about the framework nervously. "You came upon me so silently, I didn't know you were there. You startled me. I wasn't awake."

"I'm sorry," he began, as if by rote — and all at once she had the strange feeling that he had no notion still what sorrow meant. "I made you lose your fish."

"It doesn't matter," said Caribou. "We have enough fish." She knelt to pull the line of caught fish from the water, then started past him up the bank. "Let's go home."

"But it's not yet twilight."

Caribou did not answer, strode on toward the lodge not daring to look behind. Relief flooded her as she heard the boy was following, hurrying to keep up. But as they cleaned and dried the fish that afternoon, Reindeer was even more silent than usual, and Caribou did not try to draw him out. She stared down at her work and said nothing.

That evening after supper, when the boy sat on the hearthstone staring into the fire, Caribou took out the little disk of silver glass that had been her father's wedding present to her mother, and which she had not looked in for many years.

Holding it aslant so that it showed the hearth across the room, she looked at it now. With her own eyes she saw Reindeer, the boy, but the mirror showed no boy — only a reindeer calf lounging beside the fire.

A tremor passed through her. Her hands shook. So it had not been the water-sprite at all. She closed her eyes against the terror that rose in her, and tried desperately to think. *Am I going mad?* No. She shook her head. Not madness, but a terrible mystery, and she wanted no part of it.

Caribou tightened her fingers around the glass. She would not let this strange riddle into her house. She would not seek to answer it. She would not let it touch either her or Reindeer. Quietly, she put the mirror away. The next day she sent Reindeer off through the woods to a far-off slope to gather medicine-flower, and broke the mirror into slivers, then buried them between two roots of a tree.

Afterward, she told Reindeer no more tales. She herself did all their fishing in the quiet pools, though Reindeer fished the foaming rapids. Caribou painted the bottoms of all her water vessels white with bone enamel so that they would be too pale to show an image.

Her *mar long,* the only blade she had burnished bright enough to reflect images, she kept firmly in its sheath when Reindeer was with her, and she warned him away from still, standing water, telling him that it was treacherous. They still went to the hot pool to bathe, but those waters were always milky with steam, so she did not fear.

Reindeer seemed to take no notice of these changes. She had watched him at first for any reaction, but his great unchanging eyes seemed unable to evidence any mood. He did not complain. Only once did he reveal that he had noticed a difference: one morning when he was ten summers old and she was warning him for the second time to stay away from clear, dark water while hunting.

"Why is that?" he asked her. "Why are you so afraid? There is something, Cari, that you are not telling me."

Caribou felt the inexplicable terror sweeping over her again. She shook her head. "No. No, there is nothing," and pretended to be busy with the birchroot she was paring. "It is only . . ."

He said nothing, so that she had to look at him. The fear had changed to a kind of rigor. She did not think she could have stood if she had tried. Her eyes, she knew, entreated him, though she doubted he could understand.

"Reindeer, I . . ." She almost told him. "It is only that I do not want to lose you."

He stared at her intently then, for a space of several breaths, with his golden eyes. Caribou dropped her gaze. She could not tell him. She had only a terrifying suspicion buried so deep down that she herself scarcely knew what it was she feared.

Reindeer took his bow from the table then and went off into the forest to hunt, while Caribou dropped her face to her hands and moaned. She sat a long time, motionless, before the trembling passed.

6

Trangl

THE BOY came to her one day in early fall. He had seen his thirteenth summer and was nearly as tall as Caribou now. He had been restless for many days, so she knew the reindeer were running — though they had not yet returned from their summer calving grounds, for the arrow pointed away from the Pole and still Reindeer stared off northward in the evenings. But they were coming. She could tell from his manner that they would pass by soon.

"Cari," he said, "there is something I must tell you." His voice was changing, cracked unexpectedly now and again.

Caribou looked up from the candles she was dipping. "What thing, Reindeer?" she asked.

"Cari," he said quietly, "I want to go away."

Tallow spattered on Caribou's hand as she dropped the wooden candleframe into the heated kettle, and she winced. Reindeer took the iron tong from beside the hearth and fished the framework out for her.

"Go away?" she exclaimed.

Reindeer handed her the wax-coated frame; she took it gingerly. He gazed off across the room, breathed restlessly.

"Because the reindeer are running. I want to follow them and see what lies beyond the Burning Plain."

"Beyond?" cried Caribou, gripping the waxy frame till her knuckles whitened and her fingers made impressions in the soft tallow. "There lies only death beyond the Burning Plain."

The boy shook his head, still looking off. "Not for the reindeer, and not for me."

Caribou clapped the framework to the hearth-stones, shoved it away. "Why do you say that? How do you know?"

He turned to look at her now, his pale eyes burning in the firelight. "Because they have told me, Cari."

Caribou's heart shrank. She stared at him, and drew back from him, and was afraid.

"Every year at their running they call to me and tell me of sweet pastures beyond the Land of Broken Snow, and beg me to come with them."

The breath in Caribou's breast grew still then, and for a long time she could not answer him. Her thoughts spun. She felt feverish. What was he talking of — speaking with the wild deer? "Why do you want to leave me?" she whispered at last.

He shook his head and knelt upon the hearthstone by her. "I do not *want* to leave you. Each year I have refused them, till now."

"Then why now?" she whispered. She scarcely grasped what he was saying.

His tone grew warmer. "Because now I am grown tall enough and strong enough to make the trek." He laid his hands upon her hands. They felt cool against her skin. "Cari, I would ask you to come with me, but the reindeer will not let you come. I have asked them. They do not want you. Only me."

Caribou's hands curled into fists. "But you cannot go!" she burst out, gazing at him, both angry and beseeching at once. "You are just a boy, not yet a man . . ."

Reindeer took his hands from her, stood back and looked away. "Cari, I will never be a *man*. We both know it."

None of this could be happening. She clenched her teeth against the fear thickening her throat. It was a dream. "Why do you say that? What do you mean?"

He looked at her again, with his great gold eyes. "Cari, I am not like you. I am not like the others, the people who come to you and ask advice."

"Them!" cried Caribou. "Why do you listen to them, their muttering — what do they know?"

He looked at her. "More than you, in some things," he said softly.

Caribou caught in her breath. "We . . . we are not different," she stammered, stumbling on the words. "You are not different — not from *me*. I suckled you." Her hands were fists. "We are the same."

Reindeer shook his head and knelt beside her again, took up her hand in both of his. "How can you say that — why deny it? It is the difference you have been hiding from me since that day beside the stream."

Caribou felt her throat closing tight. It was no dream.

"I have seen my shadow," said the boy. "Have you never noticed it?" She shook her head, mute, staring at him. His shadow! She had not once thought of it. "It isn't like yours, a human shape. Mine is different."

Caribou blanched and closed her eyes, leaned back against the mantel stones. Her body felt wavery, thin as water. She did not want to hear any more.

"And when I listen and talk to the birds and the animals," Reindeer was saying, "you act as though you do not hear it. So many things are different between us. You laugh and you cry, and I don't understand."

Caribou's breast heaved, but she could get no air.

"And Caribou, look at this," said Reindeer. "Cari, look."

His hands left hers and her fear suddenly sharpened. She sat up quickly, snapped open her eyes, half expecting to find him vanished. But he was still beside her, had drawn his *ca'xat* from his belt and pressed its edge to the fleshy part of his palm. Caribou saw a line of gold well up. He wiped and sheathed the knife again, held up his hand to her.

"See, Cari; it's not like yours," said Reindeer. "It's gold."

Caribou felt her body slipping. The room grew dark and distorted. The firelight to the right of her tipped far away and vanished. A brief rush of cooler air brushed her. Her left arm and shoulder struck something hard. Then her cheek. She closed her eyes, because she did not want to see anymore.

"Cari," she heard him saying. "Caribou."

She found herself laid upon the hearth, the wax kettle pushed out of the way on its swinging arm, back over the coals. The heat of the close fire made her sweat. The stones against her back were uneven and hard.

She saw Reindeer above her dimly. He was bending over her, shaking her. The shaking made her gasp, and the air coming suddenly into her throat again made things grow sharper and steadier. She pushed away from Reindeer, swinging her legs to the floor, and sat up. Then she put one hand to her head and leaned against him.

"What happened?" he asked her. "Why did you do that?"

"I don't know," she muttered. She felt dizzy. Her tongue and lips were slow. "I don't understand."

"You looked like a hare that has been frightened to death," said Reindeer. His tone, oddly flat, seemed to express neither worry nor distress.

He is like a comet, or a running stream, she thought, *that has no thought for anything but itself and its own path.*

Reindeer said, "You looked like something dead in the snow. I laid you on the hearthstone to warm you."

Caribou straightened and took several quick, deep breaths. The room steadied. Her head grew clearer. "I fainted," she told him, "because I forgot to breathe."

"Did I make you do that?" he asked her. "Did I frighten you?"

She did not answer, did not look at him. She took his wounded hand that still bled slightly, drops of gold, and stared at it.

"There is something I have not told you," she said quietly. "There is something I have never told you."

She held his hand in her lap and gazed off across the twilit room.

"You are the child of my fair-sister, but not my brother's child. She brought you to me when you were newly born, just two months old, and gave you to me for safekeeping. But a great golden stag caught you out of my arms — that fall, when the reindeer were running — and carried you away in his horns. My brother killed the stag, but died himself to do it. When I came upon the two of you, the stag was bleeding drops of gold."

The boy beside her nodded. "Yes, I remember that."

Caribou turned to stare at him, his fine, fair features catching the firelight. Reindeer nodded again.

"I remember from the time the other, that other woman, brought me to you. She was my mother, I think, but she was afraid of me. And I remember when the reindeer came and bore me away. He was my father, he told me, and would carry me beyond the Land of Broken Snow. But then he stumbled, and wheeled about, and struck down the man who had been chasing us. Then we went on a little way, as far as the rocks, before he lay down, saying no more to me. And then you came."

Caribou gazed at him, unmoving. "Daimon," she whispered. "Halfling. I don't know what you are."

But she did know; she understood now — as she let herself understand at last what it was she had reared, and the thing that she had feared so long: he was a *trangl,* one of the *traangol,* the golden deer-men and deer-women that ran with the wild deer.

Reindeer took his hand from hers. "Cari," he said, "I am going away to follow the reindeer."

She looked at him, drew breath. "Will you come back?"

The boy rose, shaking his head a little, shrugged. "I don't know."

Oh, he is; he is, she thought, *a daimon, a thing I cannot understand. He is beyond my grasp. I can no more hold him than I can halt the running of water, or the turning of stars.* She tried to smile then, but her face felt crusted, crushed and set like drying clay.

"Come back," she said. "I will use the time you are away to make beautiful things for you."

Reindeer said nothing. He turned from her, going to the door, and when he opened it Caribou saw that outside the sunset was burning down the whole sky to glowing coals.

"Wait," Caribou cried. "You'll take no *pisjlak,* provisions for the journey?"

The boy stepped over the threshold and said without turning, "The reindeer will show me where good forage lies. I will need no other."

"But wait," cried Caribou again, bolting to her feet, her mind racing. Desperately, she searched the room. She had to find some way to bind him, to bring him back to her. Her eye settled on the golden reindeer hide. She ran to their bed and tore it off. *He will wear this,* she told herself, *and think of me.* She went to him outside. "Take this, at least, against the cold."

But as he took it from her, with hardly a glance,

she had suddenly the odd feeling that he had never meant to leave without it. He stroked the fur.

"My thanks," the *trangl* said.

He spoke without human inflection or emotion. He had lived in her house all these dozen years and more as a guest, nothing other, and was no kith to her at all. She felt a sudden stab of something that was almost envy. What could it be like to be like him: a daimon, untouchable by love or sorrow? Without a word, he kissed her lips.

Caribou drew back, surprised, for she had never kissed him, even as a baby, nor he her. Her people were not like the River-Valley Folk, always kissing one another's mouths. His tone grew softer then, so much so that if she had not known him for a daimon that had no use for mortal cares she would have said he spoke gently.

"Perhaps I will see you again," said Reindeer, and turned away.

Caribou stood by the house door, watching him go. Her face crumpled in despair. It was useless. She could not have held him. He had never been hers to hold. The sky above was burning gold.

She saw him take the reindeer pelt from his arm as he reached the woods' edge. He threw it about his shoulders, skin-side to him, fur-side out. Then all the woods for an instant grew bright as fire, and when Caribou could see again, she could no longer find Reindeer among the trees.

She started forward with a cry and darted down the hard, frozen slope to the woods' edge below. But the woods were empty, silent, still, all the trees black and barren, as if burnt. Nothing caught her eye but a wild stag, very far off, bounding through the trees in great strides, a young rack of antlers crowning his head. The setting sun upon his pelt made it shimmer, fire-gold.

7

The Bad Year

CARIBOU took the day-cradle of the golden stag's antlers that had lain beside the fire these many years unused and began to dismantle it with a hack-blade and saw, to fashion into beautiful things for Reindeer's return. *He will come back to me,* she told herself. *He must.* That desperate hope was the only thing that kept her moving.

She made him a horn-handled knife with intricate carvings upon the haft, spoons and little prongs for spearing food. From the spatulate antler tips she made him brooches: silhouettes of falcons and running wolves. Some of the shafts she cut into buttons, or beads, or other small things.

The last thing she started to make, from the longest and heaviest shaft of either of the antlers, was a baton such as herders used to prod their caribou. But she could not bring herself to finish it, somehow. Some impulse stopped her hand.

The rest of the autumn and all winter long, she worked on these things, hardly stirring from her cabin, for there were *waijen* all around, walking and wandering, whispering — not just dancing in the distant southern sky. It was as though the fabric between the worlds had rent, and the ancestors could now pass freely across the skybridge into the land of the living again.

Whenever Caribou did go outside, she could see them. Sometimes she thought she saw her brother in the distance, walking, his bow in hand, or her father tending his caribou — they never turned when she called. She knew they must be *waijen* and not living flesh, for there was no one in these parts who owned any caribou, and the reindeer had all run away.

Caribou did not want to see them, so mostly she stayed inside, working, scarcely pausing except to build up the fire, eat a little, and sleep. But by night or by day, whenever she slept — on the hearthstone now, for warmth, since the reindeer hide was gone — she dreamed of the wild deer rushing away from her in unstoppable torrents toward the southern Pole.

And ever as she worked — sometimes hardly knowing what it was she carved — she felt a great tightness beneath her breastbone, as though her heart had been torn out, the wound now clenching and closing over, stiff and sore. Sometimes she noticed drops of water falling onto her handiwork, as she rasped and whittled, polished and hacked, though she was barely aware that she wept.

One morning her father's *wajn* came to her. Though she did not look up, she could feel its presence filling the *ntula,* and though it did not speak, she could hear its thoughts.

You did not love him enough, my girl. That is why he has gone away.

Caribou stared down, clenching the bit of bone that she was carving. "I loved him," she whispered, then almost shouted, "I love him!"

Not enough, the *wajn's* thoughts replied. But when she looked up with a start that felt oddly like waking, no one and nothing was there.

The cold season dragged on. By day, the wan sun seemed barely to clear the horizon. The nights were interminably long. Winter storms blew in, lasting for many days. Occasionally, when the tearing wind outside her cabin dropped to eerie stillness, she could hear her own voice muttering, sometimes gasping.

"He has left me. He has left me. He will never come back."

But always the fragments of antler in her lap clicked and clattered, as clearly as if someone had spoken to her, "He will come back."

"Oh, so you think he will return to you?" someone else's voice said to her one day. "Don't believe a *trangl's* bones. All daimons are capricious, and they lie."

Caribou sat up with a start, staring. A ghostly *wajn* stood across the room. *Branja.*

"It wasn't my fault I bore a *trangl's* child," Branja's *wajn* said. "The *trangl* charmed me. One look into his golden eyes and I was powerless. Now my son has done the same to you. Look at you. You are in the same state I was in when my *trangl* left me."

"That is not so; that is not so," whispered Caribou.

"Don't lie," the *wajn* said. "You love him."

"He is like my own kith." A lie. A lie. He was nothing like a son or brother to her.

"He was never yours," the *wajn* spat. "He is *my* son, and no blood kith to you at all. You only raised him."

"I suckled him," choked Caribou.

"But could not keep him."

"Go away!" shouted Caribou, lunging to her feet. She hurled the little box she had been carving at the laughing *wajn*. The golden rectangle of horn shattered against the wall across the room. Branja was no longer there.

Spring came. The fabric of the world mended and the *waijen* went home to their Land of Endless Night. The snow about the *ntula* turned to slush. Ice upon the tree limbs cracked and fell away. Caribou finished her carving and came out to look at the world again. All around her the winter was melting in a warm, storming rush.

When the first month of spring had passed, and flowers lay strewn like broken garlands on every hill, Caribou dreamed that the reindeer were coming northward again, back from the far, southern Pole. She awoke long before dawn in a passion of desperate hope and fear. As soon as there was light enough outside to see, she left her *ntula* and hurried to the hillside beside the Reindeer's Path to wait for them.

Caribou sat trembling upon the slope green with fragrant grass. She had put on her finest clothes: a shirt and smock of white caribou skin stitched with threads of blue, wine, and green. Her boots were of golden calf's hide, and her cap, of snow-owl feathers.

The weather was unseasonably warm. Her hands plucked and worried at the shoots of grass. Time passed, endlessly, until morning was just edging into noon.

She felt the tremor in the earth and heard the far thunder of their coming long before she saw. They came in a surge, thick as gray dark water, filling the bed of the glacier-trough like a sudden flood. Caribou bolted to her feet and stood scanning the sweep of silver and gray for some glint of gold.

She saw it! *Something,* still far off — a flash of tawny yellow in the sunlight peering uncertainly through the woolen clouds. The torrent swept by her. It was a stag, golden, she could see that now, though it was difficult for her to keep him in sight amid that shifting mass. He seemed to be holding to the center of the stream.

"Reindeer! Reindeer!"

She did not understand why he did not make his way toward her, toward the edge. Surely he could see her. Caribou cupped her hands to her mouth and shouted again. The clacking thunder of the herd stole her words, trampled them to nothing. She waved her arms.

The golden reindeer turned his head. He was almost level with her now, but half the width of the channel separated them. She saw his gold eyes glance through her without thought or recognition, like a hawk's eyes, like two burning stones. Caribou dropped her arms, and the golden stag rushed by her, vanished among the stampeding forms. Gray clouds swallowed up the sun.

She could not stand. She fell forward, onto her forearms, and put her forehead to the soft, cool grass. Not even desperation held her upright anymore. The earth beneath her trembled, as she herself lay trembling.

"I have lost him; I have lost him," she whispered. She could hear nothing but the pounding of the wild deer's passing, shaking the world apart. "He has forgotten me. He will not come back."

But the necklace of reindeer teeth that bit against her breast clattered softly. Strange how she could hear them still, even above the thunder of the wild deer. "He has not forgotten you. He will come back."

The cool of evening woke her, and when she rose, stiff from having lain so long, and trembling with fatigue, she saw that the herd had passed, the earth again grown still. Dusk was drawing on, the air fast giving up its heat.

Numbly, Caribou went home, and wept no more — she was worn out with it; there was nothing she could do. She locked the things she had made of the golden stag's horns away in a wooden chest, and slept that night on her own bed again, not the hearth, beneath an old coverlet of gray caribou hide, and thought no more of Reindeer.

I should never have loved him, she told herself bitterly. *I will never love anyone again.*

That was the year the people from the villages began

bringing their disputes to her, because of the repu-
tation that had sprung up around her in the last years
as a wisewoman. The chieftain over the whole Tribe
had died that winter, and his children were bickering
over who should succeed him. The elder-councils were
deadlocked as well.

So slowly at first, then more and more frequently,
the people came to her with their cases to be settled,
because they could get no satisfaction from the councils and had no tribal head to lay down for them the
Law.

Caribou heard them, and passed judgments, which
she insisted both parties agree to honor before she
would consent to hear them. Sometimes more than
one group came on a day, so that the opponents of
the first party presented their cases while those of the
other watched and listened. Always it was agreed that
her decisions were just and fair. She did not mind the
time it took. It kept her from being alone.

People still came to her for advice, or information,
or help finding lost articles as well, for still she dreamed
wise dreams of prophecy. She turned no one unanswered away, till word began to spread that the wisewoman who lived near the Broken Lands had grown
more sage and deep than ever, though rather sad now
that her nephew, or son, or younger brother — the
golden boy — had gone away to become a *kaluwak,*
a tracker who followed the wild deer.

Such was the way of things for a long year's time.
Then came the Bad Year. It started in spring, growing
worse as the months wore into summer. Caribou saw

some of it for herself, and the people who came for her judgments brought tales of it with them.

It began with tremors in the earth — though this was not unusual, in the cold country of geysers and mud-springs, for the earth to tremble now and again; at first no one had thought anything of it. But soon the shocks began to come more frequently, and were more violent, so that by the end of summer scarcely a day went by that Caribou did not feel at least a mild shudder pass through the earth.

In early fall, before the snows blocked off the passages, when people still came with their troubles and their news, she heard of worse things yet. Great cracks had been found, thirty els deep in the earth. Certain geysers had ceased to spout, others begun spouting erratically. Landslides sheared off whole sides of hills, and rivers flowed muddy, thick with debris.

Then, at mid-autumn, after the reindeer had run, Caribou made her way across the glacier-trough and through the woods to bathe in the hot pool one last time before the snows. She had not been there all summer, so often had the villagers been coming to her.

On her way to the pool, to her surprise, she found that the barren patch of warm ground in the forest had grown hotter, expanding and killing the trees that had formerly ringed it. The earth was almost too hot for her to travel across, and noxious fumes now rose from vents in the crust.

When she neared the hot spring, she discovered that it had turned a soupy yellow, with great streams of

particulated sulfur extending far over the rocky ground
where wind had blown the spray of geysers. Animal
tracks — all fleeing — showed here and there in the
thick, pollen-colored dust.

Suddenly as she approached, crunching over the
hardened crust, she realized that what she had thought
were mineral mounds beside the spring were really
the carcasses of animals, covered with sulfur, those
that had been caught drinking from the spring and
had not had time to flee.

Caribou stood staring at them, horrified. What could
have become of the water-daimon to have allowed
this to happen? She muttered a propitiation under her
breath — but before she had even half finished, she
heard a rumbling from across the little pond. A great
plume of yellow steam jetted up from a fissure in the
rock, with a spitting hiss and a stink like rotting eggs.

Caribou gasped and fell back, nearly overcome by
the heat. Surely the water-sprite was dead or driven
away, and no daimon protected this place anymore.
A gust of wind began blowing spray from the hot,
churning plume. Caribou turned and fled away over
the sulfurous earth, that crunched like yellow salt beneath her heels.

All that winter, Caribou stayed close to the lodge
but for brief forays into the near woods for hunting
or checking her traps. Sometimes during the stillness
of the night, she heard avalanches tearing apart the
mountains many miles to the east.

One morning, while she sat mending a broken snare

by the hearthside, she heard a distant booming. Rushing outside, she saw above the low slopes far to the west a dark cloud welling up from beyond the horizon's edge, mounting and spreading into the sky like a swarm of black birds. That evening, ash fell, graying the leafless trees and dirtying the snow.

It was as if all order and balance had left the world — nothing could be predicted anymore. Whereas the winter before, the earth had seemed crowded with unearthly *waijen,* now it seemed deserted, empty. Game had grown scarce. Butter would not come in the churn. There seemed to be no magic in any of the charms.

It was as if every sprite and *ont* and troll that kept the mountains and the geysers, the paths and streams, had abruptly vanished, leaving the world without keeper or guide. There was no appealing to them for luck or appeasement. The offerings Caribou left along the paths and the streams remained untouched.

Still she dreamed, but her dreams were no help. They remained blank of these things, telling her nothing. Though sometimes she felt as if she knew where every lost article lay in all the sixteen villages of her Tribe, she had no inkling why the world should be so restless and intractable.

It was at the first of spring, as soon as the passages were open again, that the elders came to her.

"We are a special council," their spokesman said, "formed of an elder from each of the sixteen villages."

They sat on blankets spread on the barren ground outside her hut. Caribou had served them honeycakes and bitter tea. She sat facing them from the threshold, the golden arrow across her lap. She liked to run her hands over its hard, cool surface while she listened. It pointed south, for the wild deer had not yet returned.

"Have the elder-councils chosen a new chieftain yet?" she inquired, sipping her tea.

The speaker shook his head. He was a man late in middle age, with hair like a silver cap upon his head and a drooping gray moustache. He came from nearby Vlad. "No, wisewoman," he told her. "Our late chieftain's children and the village councils are all quarreling still, and the events of the past winter have thrown us all into confusion."

Caribou was silent then, wondering why they had come. At length one man among the group laid down his tea-flask and brushed the crumbs from his beard.

"My name is Ksistan," he said to Caribou, "and I come from the village of Bintuk, several leagues north of here. There the shaking of the earth has been most violent — sometimes so severe it throws people to the ground and pitches down fences so our caribou run wild-eyed and screaming till the shaking stops."

A woman spoke. She was from the village of Bora, she said. Caribou could tell that even before she spoke, by the red *pistra*-shawl about her shoulders.

"Our water-sprites are dead, wisewoman. All the wells of our villages have been poisoned with red rust," she told her. "Even the river is fouled. We have to climb the mountain every day for water, to the high springs where the hot jets have grown unpredictable. Already three of our people have been killed, and many more spattered and scalded."

She held out her wrist so Caribou could see the burn-welt across the palm and forearm.

Another woman came forward, with thick gray hair that had once been black, plaited into braids with beads in them, like the River-Valley People wore, but her skin was olive, not tan, and her eyes were dark, not green.

"I am Brikka," she told Caribou, "and my village lies on the high slopes, steep above the Huëndl River. A village of Valley Folk used to lie below us. But when the great mountain to the west of us burst apart — you saw the smoke? Cinders fell on us."

"Here, too," Caribou answered, lifting a palmful of soil from the ground beside her, made grayer by fine ash. "But what happened to the Valley Folk?"

"The ashfall did no great damage," the woman Brikka continued, "either to our own village or to theirs. No one was killed. But the shock of the explosion shook free the cliffs beside the Forbidden Caves, below our village and to the south of us. Again, no one was harmed.

"But during the night, we surmise, some heavy ether — tasteless, odorless — seeped from the broken slope and down into the valley below us, poisoning the air. In the morning we saw Valley People stagger from their houses and fall dead. We were afraid to go to them. Some of our cattle wandered too far down the slopes and also died."

Caribou's skin prickled as she listened. She gripped

the arrow in her lap. She had never heard of such a thing before. The elder with the beads in her hair went on.

"This was two months ago. We have tried offerings and propitiations to every daimon we know, but nothing avails. The valley below us is sheltered, but sometimes when a strong wind sweeps through from the southeast, blowing hard for half a day, the valley is safe to venture into for a few hours' time.

"But as soon as the wind stills, we must climb the slopes at once, or perish. We have floated messages of warning to villages downstream, but as yet no one has brought any reply. We think the river-daimons have stolen our messages, or else the Valley People have already fled in their barges to the sea."

One by one the council members came forward, each in turn telling Caribou his or her tale of disaster. When they were done, Caribou sat speechless. Alone all winter in her *ntula,* cut off from the rest of her Tribe, she had had no idea of the extent of the calamity. She gazed at the drawn and worried faces of the councillors.

"Surely all of this is horrible," she managed at last. "But . . . why come to me? What am I to do?"

"We have come to you," their spokesman Djenret said, "O wisest of women, to ask what daimons are angry with us. Or is it our *waijen* we must propitiate? And how? You are a seer and a dreamer of dreams. Surely you must know."

But Caribou only shook her head. She felt as puzzled as he. "No daimons are angry with you, as far as I can see. Nor is it your ancestors who protest some slight. You have offended no one."

"Is it the earth, then?" ventured a woman with the pleated smock of a mountain goatherd. "Have we ill-used the earth somehow, that it heaves and groans to snuff us out?"

Again Caribou shook her head. "I have had no dreams of that." She had had no dreams of any of it, or none that she could recall.

"Is it . . . ?" a man near the back of the group began. "Is it then, truly, the end of the world, as our village shaman has said — there is no escaping the destruction?"

Caribou sighed deeply and said to him, "I cannot believe the earth is dying. Fire and steam are part of the earth and do it no damage. They only harm people and animals, and green growing things."

She paused a moment, frowning and thinking. There must be an answer to it, somehow, somewhere.

"But as for why this trembling of the earth has come, or where the magic and the daimons have gone, I have no answer yet."

She sighed, glancing toward the western horizon, which was smoldering to dusk. Never before had anyone laid such a task upon her. She was keenly aware that whatever answer she gave would affect the whole of her Tribe.

"Will you give me one night to dream on it?" she asked of them. "In the morning, I will tell you what I can recommend."

She rose. The elders bowed their heads respectfully,

accepting her words, but she could see they were surprised, and not at all satisfied that she would not answer them at once. She herself felt pained and weary.

"Very well, *i'dris,*" their leader told her — it was a name they had begun to call her, for they considered her a seer. "We will camp away from your *ntula,* at wood's edge, so that our campfires and our councils will not disturb you."

She offered them food for the night, but they said they had brought their own. They gathered up their blankets and went away, and Caribou went inside the hut. She was troubled still. Not in all her years as a wisewoman had she turned anyone away unanswered, even for a night.

And thinking now, very deep, she began to recall the barest edges of dreams, dreams that she had forgotten immediately upon waking: of the upheavals in the earth and the raining destruction, and all the daimons moving off southward in a great troup, toward the Pole and the spirit world, the Land of Everlasting Night.

She concentrated deeply, desperately. But not one dream, now only fleetingly recalled, gave her any inkling of what was causing the disorder, or how to bring the daimons back or halt the rending of the world.

Caribou shook herself. Her head was aching now, and she had achieved nothing. Slowly, she took off her smock and shirt and set her boots and leggings at the foot of her bed. She was very tired, and would doubtless dream truer sleeping than awake. At last she crawled beneath the coverlet of gray caribou skins and, though restless and uneasy still, soon drifted into sleep.

A soft scratching at the door awakened her in the dark. The night was still. She could hear someone's impatient breathing, short snorts, just outside the door. Caribou got up from the bed and wrapped the caribou skins around her, shaking with cold.

What could the councillors want at such an hour? She had not dreamed yet, even one dream that night, and they had said that they would not disturb her. Caribou sighed and relented a little then. Perhaps they had let their coals die, and needed fire.

She padded barefoot across the soft, cool skins on the floor, and laid her hand upon the latch. As she did so, a brilliant light shone for an instant outside. Its brightness dazzled her, even through the cracks. Caribou started, shielding her eyes. She had seen such a brightness only once before.

Heaving up the latch, she hauled open the door. A fair-skinned youth stood on the threshold, not more than sixteen summers old. He had wheat-colored hair and golden eyes. A robe of golden reindeer pelt lay over his arm. He did not tremble with the cold, only gazed on her, his eyes revealing neither joy nor sorrow.

8

The Wild Deer

CARIBOU stood in her doorway, clutching the caribou robe about her, and stared at Reindeer. It had been two years and a half since he had gone away. She could hardly believe the change in him. He was no longer a boy . . . But what was he doing here? The question panged in her suddenly. Why had he returned to her now, after all this time?

"They wanted me to stay with them," he told her, speaking without hesitation — as though he had never been away — "the wild deer. They wanted me to run with them forever over the frozen plain." The night was dark and chill. She shivered again. The *trangl* shook his head. "But I could not. I have wanted to return for many months. And so at last, this season, I came away."

Caribou could say nothing, could only gaze at him. He was taller than she was now, his golden hair longer and untrimmed, his voice deeper. A few silk strands of unshaven beard pricked the smooth skin of his cheeks, but that was all. Somehow she knew he would never have more beard than that. He was not a man. His golden eyes were exactly as she remembered them.

"There are some people camped near here, at the

woods' edge," he said after a moment. "I saw their fires, and waited until they were asleep."

Caribou nodded and found that she, too, could speak now, almost naturally. "Yes, I know. They came about the failing geysers, the trembling ground, and the great upheavals in the earth."

"What trembling?" Reindeer asked. "What upheavals in the earth?"

"Come inside," she told him, shaking, "and I will say."

She held back the door, and when he had entered, she shut it. Reindeer knelt beside the hearth, made up the fire with kindling and an iron tong while Caribou took a sash to tie the caribou robe. Then she brought him food, which he ate willingly, almost ravenously.

"I have not tasted human food these many months," he said, "since I was gone from you."

Caribou knelt beside the hearth as well, partly for warmth, but mostly to be near him. She was shivering still. "You leapt away from me," she said softly, "that first spring when the reindeer came back. I stood on the hillside of the Reindeer's Path and watched for you, but you rushed on with the others. Why? After that, I never looked for you."

The youth laid down his bowl, and now, it seemed, he hesitated. "I did not want to remain away from you," he said at last. His fathomless eyes sometimes looked at her, and sometimes down. "The others urged me to it. They said the pain would pass — but it did not pass."

His fingers touched hers upon the hearth.

"You told me once, Cari, that you feared I had no human heart. Perhaps that is so. I am not a man. But heart I have; that much I know, for it ached after that, very sorely, like a wound. Sometimes it eased a little, or I forgot the pain, but always it returned, more and more strongly."

Caribou smiled then, a little smile. Her fingers closed over his. It had been a long time since she had touched him. The joy in her was so great it was almost pain.

"My eyes stung," the young man said.

He looked off across the darkened room as if puzzled. Then he caught her hand suddenly, and his golden eyes catching the firelight, burned bright as meteors.

"How can I tell you what it was like, Cari? Running with the wild deer over the Burning Plain and beyond the southern Pole. That season, that first season, was the only time I truly forgot you here, this house, and the people of this land. There were . . . such things, so *much* to see and learn."

The heat of him warmed Caribou's hand. His breath quickened. Then abruptly his expression darkened.

"They are very different from your people, are the wild deer. They know nothing of laughing and weeping, Cari, only a fierce, wild freedom in coursing the Broken Plain. They did not want to accept me at first, saying I was too old to join them, had worn a human shape too long. They said that though I now wore a reindeer's hide, I was still a man beneath the skin — too cautious and trembling and tiring, not fearsome as they are, and free."

His eyes were fixed on some far point across the room. Caribou watched him.

"They debated long. But at last I persuaded them, for my father's sake, to take me in. I told them I would never be happy among humankind, which is the truth."

He glanced at Caribou. Her fingers tightened, and her heart grew cold, hearing him, but she did not speak. He looked away.

"So they said I must forget love and sorrow, all human things, and ride with them all day without resting, over the Burning Plain, beyond the broken snow."

A little silence followed, filling the room, sifting into the cracks, like darkness falling. They sat a time, not looking or speaking to one another.

"Are they," said Caribou at last, softly, "are all of them like you — able to throw off their hides and walk in human shape?"

He shook his head. "Only the golden ones," he said. "There is a legend — a legend that our kind were human once, outcasts from your people: *kaaluwati*, who followed the reindeer. But one day they stood in a golden shower that spouts beside the Forge of the Fireking, a geyser of burning gold that transfigured them into stags and hinds."

"The Fireking," murmured Caribou. She had never heard of such a one. "Who is the Fireking?"

"The king of the firelords, the lords of the earth," Reindeer replied. "They mine deep below the ground, hunting for gold and precious silver. They came here long ago, and that is when the earth first began to be restless." He glanced at her. "They work at their forge, sweating and smelting, all night and all day."

"What do they make?" whispered Caribou, but Reindeer only shrugged.

"Who knows?"

His expression grew more solemn still. Caribou eased her grip upon his hand. Again he looked away.

"I have seen that shower," Reindeer said, "and stood in its spray. All *traangol* must bathe in it at least once, early in life — else their reindeer selves begin to fade, and die away."

Caribou felt a little twinge, thinking, *if only I could have held him a little longer, perhaps, perhaps* . . . But it was no use wishing. She said instead, "And why is that — does not the line of the golden ones breed true?"

"It does not breed at all," said Reindeer suddenly. His brusqueness startled her. "The halflings cannot conceive with one another's seed, but must return here to the country of their ancestors to lie with human women and men."

Caribou listened to him, frowning.

"The hinds carry their calves to the calving grounds to bear them in spring. Then in fall, when we pass by the Fount of Gold, they bathe them in its rain to loosen their reindeer skins so they may lay them aside at will. The stags carry off their children from their human mothers in the fall, before they have been long suckled and grown too human. Then they bathe them in the Fount to give them reindeer skins and let them run with the wild deer beyond the Burning Plain."

The youth sat looking down as he said that, picking absently at a rough place on the hearth. Caribou stirred. She was frowning still. "But it is wrong to lie with men only for the getting of children," she began.

Memory of Branja came to her, for the first time since the winter of the *waijen* and of Reindeer's leaving her. But it was not the taunting *wajn* she pictured now. Rather it was Branja as she had been in life — flinging herself before the golden stag, and clutching at Caribou's arm. Hapless Branja. Caribou's voice gained strength.

"And it is wrong to steal a woman's child when she does not want to give it up."

Reindeer shrugged and shook his head. "The *traangol* are a proud race, august and cold. They do not understand the warmer hearts of mortal creatures." He looked at her. "They bear your people no malice, Cari, and take from you only what they need."

Caribou drew back from him. His flat, dispassionate tone still had the power to surprise her. "Perhaps," she answered softly, "but still they *take* from my people what is not freely offered. And that is wrong."

He sighed, and stubbed his thumb and forefinger against the roughened stone. Almost, it seemed, he was smiling at her with his golden eyes, till she wondered, How human was he — or did she only imagine it? He took her hand again.

"Come tell them so yourself, then, Cari," he told her. "You are very wise. I have no doubt you could find words to make the wild deer listen."

For a moment she could not speak. "What are you saying?" she whispered. She had not intended the words to be so soft.

"I want you to come back with me," said the golden-eyed young man, "when the reindeer run southward in the fall. I will carry you upon my back as far as the Fount. There you can bathe in its spray and become a *trangl,* like me, and run with me among the wild deer by winter and spring."

Caribou gazed at him dismayed. She saw the fire that had come into his face, heard the expectation with which he spoke, as though already certain what her answer would be. But what he wanted filled her with fear. She was a mortal woman, and had no *trangl*'s blood in her, like Reindeer, yearning to join the wild deer.

She said nothing. A space of silence then. The room grew very still. No wind, no wolf, no *wajn* whispered at the door. The fire was dying down. Caribou took her hand from his and threw another piece of kindling on the fire. She sighed.

"If you had come last night," she began, "but one day earlier, perhaps . . . perhaps I could have gone with you. But now — now I cannot."

She glanced at him and saw that his face had paled and fallen. Did she detect somehow upon those unearthly features a sadness? She could not be sure. The sense of desperation and futility that had gripped her only hours before returned. She thought of the councillors outside, dozing beside their campfires at the woods' edge.

"Those people you saw camped below," she told him, unable to keep the urgency from her voice anymore, "they have asked my aid, not only for themselves, but for all the villages of my Tribe. There have been great changes in the earth since you left, great geysers of fire and the hotlands spreading."

Briefly, she told him what she knew.

"I am afraid. All my people will perish if I do not help them." *But how?* Fatigue nibbled at her. She could not think. "Is the earth dying? Why have the daimons gone away?"

And Reindeer replied, almost indifferently, "The firelords are turning the earth, for they have mined all the gold and precious silver they can find here. The daimons know this. That is why they have gone."

Caribou stared at him. "Turning the earth — what do you mean?"

"They are making it new," he told her, "reshaping it, like a *trangl* throwing its skin, so that in time it will make new gold and silver for them."

Whatever she thought she had seen in his face a moment before had vanished. She could not fathom his calm. That he could speak of such things, such incomprehensible things, so easily! Surely he was a daimon — how could she ever have mistaken him for a man?

"But what are my people to do?" Caribou said desperately. "How may we live where the earth is changing, without our daimons to protect us?"

Again she thought of the councillors. She had promised to dream on it and give them their answer at dawn. But she had had no dreams that night, or none she could recall.

Reindeer said, "I know of a place where the firelords do not come, where the earth is not restless."

Caribou turned, her weariness once more overcome by surprise. Something seemed to have rekindled in him.

"It is the wintering ground of the wild deer," the golden young man told her, "and lies beyond the Pole."

Then Caribou's heart closed up, and she tore her gaze away, certain suddenly that he was mocking her. "Beyond the Pole?" she hissed. "That is the way the *waijen* go, to their Country of Endless Night."

"Not so," the *trangl* said. "Sweet lands of forest lie there, and green grass growing."

"But none may pass so far south," she said. "The cold . . ."

He shook his head. "The reindeer pass."

"And how may one follow the reindeer?" she asked bitterly, hardly listening, angry at his mocking her, "that run more swiftly than a bird can fly?"

"The caribou may follow," the young man upon the hearthstone said. "They are near cousins of the wild deer, and almost as fleet. And your people may follow, too, if they will, for I can build you a thing, a kind of boat that skates upon the land. It is drawn by another kind of deer than reindeer, though caribou could draw it."

Caribou stood listening.

Reindeer said, "I have seen such a thing on the other side of the world. I put off my *trangl*-skin at the edge of our wintering grounds this winter past, to help a girl and her brother repair their boat, whose runner had broken. They showed me how to guide it."

She searched his face, but it told her nothing. Could her people use such things as he described to escape the fire and storm of the firelords' turning of the earth? He was a daimon. He would know such things. But what had Branja's *wajn* said? *All daimons are capricious, and they lie.*

Could she trust him? In all his years with her, Reindeer had never done anything to cause her to doubt him — yet he had been with the wild deer since then, and learned their ways. Caribou shoved such thoughts aside and made up her mind. She had no choice.

"What is needed for the building of these boats that skate upon the land?" she asked.

"Not much," he said. "Only wood, and sinew for binding, and reins."

"Are they difficult to build or hard to sail?"

Again he shook his head, and she swore that in another moment he would smile. She had come to stand very near him, less than an arm's reach away. She could feel his breath upon the air.

"Then I will tell the councillors tomorrow," she answered. "And we will build our landships to be away across the southern Pole as soon as may be."

He put his hands on her arms to draw her closer. "Not quite so soon. We must wait until fall. Only then is the Burning Plain solid enough to bear the weight of our passage. Landships must have hard, frozen ground to skate upon."

"Fall?" whispered Caribou, suddenly fearful. She thought of the worsening fury of the earth all that winter past and shuddered. "Do we have so long?"

Reindeer nodded, but she wondered if even a daimon could know such a thing with certainty. She avoided his eyes, and managed to draw away from him. She went to her storing chest.

"Let me show you the things I made for you from your cradle-antlers," she said, and brought some of them to him beside the fire: the horn-hafted knife, the brooches and buttons, cuff-clasps and needles, the unfinished baton.

He knelt and looked at them all very carefully in the firelight, picking each up and fingering it before laying it down. Finally he looked at her, saying solemnly, "These are all very fine, beautifully made. But I have no use for them. I am a *trangl*."

Caribou closed her eyes, for her eyelids stung fiercely. She refused to think of it — refused to think of his putting on his *trangl*-skin and going away from her again. "But you may use them while you remain with me, and wear your man-shape," she whispered, beseeching. "Take them."

He nodded, and then just for a moment his unreadable expression seemed to soften, to change. Could she be seeing him right? The flickering of the embers was dim and full of shadows. He took his hand from the carved things on the hearth and hesitated, then reached to touch her face.

"If I take your people to a safe land," he asked her, very gently, "far from burning earth and spouting fire, will you then come with me, and run beside me with the wild deer?"

She wanted to shake her head or turn away from him, but she could not. His flesh was warm against the bone of her cheek, and her own hands very cold. His golden eyes were searching hers. She felt a flash of something hot darting through her then, and thought of Branja's *wajn* again, for she found that at that moment she could neither say nor do anything Reindeer did not want.

She told him, "Yes."

He drew her to him, and kissed her forehead and eyes. The heat of him, and the strength of his arms encircling her made Caribou's knees weak. She put her own arms about his neck to keep from falling.

"My people will not welcome you," he whispered, "but I do not fear for you at all. They do not understand why I long for the company of a human creature. But in the end they will admire you, as I do. I know it."

His breath had a sweet taste, like new grass growing. She gasped for breath.

"If they so disapprove of me already," she managed, "why ever did they let you go?"

"I told them," he answered — did his eyes laugh? Did they smile? — "that I must go among my mother's people again to find me a mate and get me a child."

Her hands upon his shoulders tightened. "Is that the reason you have returned to me?" she wondered, and did not realize she had spoken aloud until he answered, "Yes."

Caribou's heart grew cold then, even as he kissed her mouth. *I know beyond all hope of saving that I love you,* she thought, *but do you love me? You are not mortal. Can you love?* It made not the slightest bit of difference, for she had looked into his daimon's eyes.

9

Boats That Skate
upon the Land

THAT DAWN Caribou rose, put on her shirt and smock and boots, wrapped her heavy *lanlan* about her, and walked down to the camp of the elders to speak with them. She found them already awake and looking as if they, too, had not slept much the night before.

They eyed her strangely, and seemed much more reticent than they had been the previous day. Now and again, their glances strayed to her *ntula*. Caribou told them of the firelords, letting them believe she had learned of them in a dream. Then she told them to go back to their villages and be of good heart, for very soon — within the month — she would come down from the Wilderland with a means to save them from the changing of the earth.

The councillors rose, gathering their possessions, and went away — but with much soft murmuring among themselves and much furtive glancing back through the trees toward Caribou and the cabin on the bare rise behind her. Some of them whispered that they had dreamed of a golden light shining through the woods the night before. Some said the wisewoman had called a *trangl* to consult with her, while others said the *trangl* always came.

She overheard a little of their talk and almost laughed, for she felt lightheaded with lack of sleep and with joy at Reindeer's return. She loved him. Nothing else mattered. When at last the elders were gone, Caribou turned and went back to lie the rest of the morning with her golden daimon, dozing and talking with him.

He built the landboat, as he had promised her, hewing the hard-grained ash trees down with the antler-hafted ax she had made him. He split the timbers and planed them smooth, shaping them, then fitted them with dovetailing and pegs.

She, meanwhile, on his instruction, slit out and braided cords and cords of leather thong. These he used to reinforce the joints and lash the runners underneath the belly, after he had shod them with gold by running a little of his blood all down their length.

"Why have you done that?" Caribou asked him, coming out of the house to bring him more thong. Reindeer nodded toward the gold-smeared runners already drying in the cool spring breeze.

"To point them always toward where the reindeer are," he replied, "like that arrow that you keep."

And when the landboat at last was done and the gilded runners lashed into place, he called it a *gristal,* for that was the name the two young strangers he had rescued had called theirs. It rode low to the ground and was narrow, less than a woman's arm-span across, with a substantial hold in front, deceptively shallow-seeming, in which gear and supplies could be packed.

Near the back was space for one or more passengers to sit, one behind the other on top of the baggage, and behind that, a running board for one to stand upon and drive the sledge, using a willow switch and a pair of thongs, called reins, for guiding.

Once the *gristal* itself was made, Reindeer set about fashioning a padded collar of strong, supple leather stuffed with fur, that a draft-deer might pull the sledge, while Caribou braided more strips and stitched together bands of leather for making what Reindeer told her would form the harness and traces.

Each thing he did, he showed her carefully how it was done and let her try it, so that she would know exactly how it had been accomplished and could instruct the others of her Tribe.

She and Reindeer worked hard each day outside while the light lasted and late into the evenings by the hearthside at night, then lay in each other's arms beneath the fur of the reindeer robe, till dawn. The spring moons dwindled and grew fat, and by day Caribou felt that she had never been more happy. No people came at all that month to trouble them. She and her *trangl* were left alone.

The earth still trembled beneath their feet, often violently, and sometimes in the west they saw dark haze that turned the sunset sepia. But it all seemed very distant from her now, and at times Caribou felt her heart swell nearly to bursting with contentment as she worked beside her golden young man.

At night, though, her sense of well-being faded. Sometimes she and Reindeer heard the crash of mountains falling far away, and felt the tremors. She dreamed then, terrible dreams that made her toss, moaning and muttering, until Reindeer shook her awake, saying, "What is it? What is it — are you in pain?"

"No," Caribou told him once, sitting up beneath the reindeer robe. The cold night air rushed in around her. "No, I had a nightmare."

She put the heel of one hand to her eye to scrub the sleep away, brushed back a loose strand of hair. Sleep drained from her in a pungent prickle. She glanced at Reindeer, but he seemed puzzled still.

"A . . . kind of vision," she murmured. "All smoke and burning."

"Tell me," he said, putting his arms around her and lying back down with her against him. The reindeer fur settled on top of them again.

"I saw," she sighed, remembering, "that it was evening; all the air was filled with choking smoke. I saw you standing in your man-shape. Your hair was a golden fire that lit up the night and did not harm you. Then you vanished, and all was darkness again.

"Suddenly there were people all around me, running and screaming. I could hear the caribou snorting, stampeding, and I could hear bells. Dimly, I saw people trying to flee through the woods, but the trees were all alight. Some of the people were trying to escape over a bare rocky place, away from the trees, but the earth broke apart, and the rocks melted into a slow liquid fire."

She shook her head, shuddering. Her voice was shuddering as well.

"Still others were poling in barges downriver toward the sea. I have never seen the sea, but in the dream it looked like open tundra, flat and gray — save that when the barges reached it, the water began to heave and boil, sending up great gouts of steam like white plumes into the air. They swamped the boats, and the people pitched into the water and drowned.

"And the last people I saw had run to the tops of the highest hills to pray to the moons to succor them. But Greatmoon floated above them, dull copper in the heavens, stripped of its brightness, and Littlemoon lay pale and thin upon the far horizon. Only those people who had followed the sound of the bells got safe away."

She did not realize that she had begun to weep until she felt Reindeer touching her damp cheeks, then saw him holding his fingers up to look at the tears there in the dull glow of the hearth. His face bore the same impassive, perplexed look he always wore whenever she laughed or wept. She held him closer, and he put his arms around her once again.

"We will go down to the first of the villages tomorrow," he told her, "and you can show them how to build *gristaal* and how to drive them."

"Tomorrow?" Caribou asked him. "But . . . what will I say to them? I have had no time to prepare —"

Reindeer took her hand. "When have you ever needed more than a moment to consider your words?" he asked, in a tone that, if he had been human, would have sounded chiding. "You will speak to your people as you always have, telling them all they need to know. And they will listen."

She was not so sure. Uncertainty nagged at her. Would her people trust her tale of the firelords — strange beings they had never heard of before? Would they follow her advice to build sledges and flee? Another thought occurred to her.

"But how can we go tomorrow?" she asked. "We haven't any caribou to pull the sledge, and no *pisjlak* laid in."

"Never mind about supplies," Reindeer replied. "The villagers will supply you with all."

Caribou looked at him, more puzzled now. His face had no expression, like a *wajn*'s, like an owl's. She did not question him.

"And do not worry about the caribou. I will pull your sledge."

Caribou felt her heart grow small. She laid her head against his shoulder. "You'll not come down in man-shape to the villages?"

He shook his head. "Let them wonder who and what I am." He ran his hand along her shoulder a moment, absently. "Besides, if I go man-disguised, who will teach the caribou to draw the sledges?"

She put her hand on his and closed her eyes, telling herself his distance was not strange to her. He had always been so — and after so many months without him, his presence alone should comfort her. She would not think of anything else. Soon sleep welled up around her in his arms, and she dreamed no more until morning.

At first light, they rose and loaded the sledge with what little food was on hand. There were hardly any of the winter stores left, and they had both been too busy to lay in new. Then they shut up the house.

The sledge rode light. Even Caribou, who had not driven the *gristal* before, could tell as she stood upon the driver's step, bundled in her *lanlan* against the wind, how easily the craft bucked and skipped across the slick, muddy ground, through the last of the slushy snow, the runners sparking when they hit a stone.

Reindeer had thrown off the new man-clothes Caribou had made him, thrown on his golden deer-pelt, skin-side to his skin, and now ran between the traces, drawing the sledge behind him. Caribou was dazzled at their downhill speed. Not even in dreams had she ever flown so swift.

They ran through noon, into the afternoon, coming into the first village just at dusk. People ran to them and cried in wonder, reaching to touch — yet not quite touch — the sleek wooden craft, the strange golden deer.

"What marvel is this," they cried, "that skims over land light as a bird through air, *i'dris?*"

Caribou reined in her Reindeer — gently, gently — let the landboat slide to a stop before the main hall of the village just as the village elders emerged and stood, wide-eyed, upon the porch. *They are more speechless than I,* she thought, relieved, and felt her confidence beginning to return.

Amid the crowd of their strange faces, she noted one that was familiar, the spokesman of the special council that had come to her. Caribou searched her memory, then smiled.

"Hail, Djenret of Vlad," she called. "Why so amazed? Did I not say I would come within the month with the means to rescue us from this unsettled place?"

"Welcome, *i'dris,*" the councillor replied, regaining himself a little after his surprise. "Will you come into our council hall and tell us of this thing?"

He and the rest of the elders fell back then as Caribou brought Reindeer and the *gristal* right up the steps and into the hall. Her nervousness had vanished now. Inside, she talked to the elders and as many of the villagers as could crowd into the room. She spoke of the firelords' changing of the earth, which had driven all the daimons away.

As darkness fell, bonfires were lit in the streets outside and the great hearths stoked within. Meat and drink were brought to refresh the wisewoman, and sweet hay for her golden stag. Those villagers who could not fit into the hall crowded about the unshuttered windows, wrapped in furs, or gossiped and sipped hot ale about the bonfires or upon the porch, wondering about the wisewoman and her godlike car, and the wild golden deer that drew it.

Caribou explained the workings of the sledge and the means for its construction. She described the felling and splitting of the wood, the shaping and shaving, the fitting of joints to be both strong and flexible, the lashing of runners and their waxing with beeswax.

She told them of the land beyond the Burning Plain, that she had dreamed of and been told of by one who had followed the wild deer there and back again — she let them think what they would of that — and how, come fall, they must follow the wild herds across the Pole to the other side of the world, or perish.

When at last the evening had grown so late and still that none felt they could hold open their eyes a moment more, people within the hall stretched out where they were and huddled beneath their *lanlani* beside the great fireplaces. Those outside who had gotten places beside the bonfires sat nodding by the warmth, while those who had not retreated to the shelter of their houses for the few hours till dawn.

The day broke — too soon, it seemed to Caribou. She awakened, astonished to hear the ring of axes and the fall of timber through the woods as people, already up, were even now felling trees for the construction of sledges. All day, while the wood-shapers and carpenters worked, Caribou showed the others how to braid and stitch the harness-lines, how to fashion them into halters and bridles, how to pad the harness-straps with fur.

That night, exhausted again, she slept in the best guesthouse, quartered there at the villagers' insistence — and nothing half so fine had she ever seen in all her life. The walls of her chamber were paneled and decorated with carvings, and there were candles of beeswax and soap that foamed like beer yet bore the strong, sweet scent of roses.

Reindeer they had corraled with the village caribou, where he waited patiently until late evening when every soul, or nearly, was asleep; then he leapt the high-railed fence in a bound and pawed softly at Caribou's window. She opened the shutters, and he threw off his deerskin, coming in to lie the night with her.

They stayed six days in Vlad, till Littlemoon was new again. Caribou showed the people how to pack the landboats properly, wedging the stores in, lashing them down, laying the weight evenly and taking care not to overload the hold. She showed many of them how to drive a sledge, using her own, letting them handle the reins and guide Reindeer — gently, always gently — where they wished to go.

"You must train your teams for stamina," she said to Djenret, "for by fall they must be able to run for hours at a stretch."

While Caribou helped the people fashion their sledges, Reindeer mingled with their caribou, singing them the songs the golden ones had taught him, teaching them all they would need to know to draw the sledges across the Burning Plain and follow the reindeer over the Pole.

On the seventh day, she and Reindeer left Vlad. The building of the *gristaal* was well underway, and she knew by the growing number of strangers coming into town to stare at her and the building that word of her landboat was spreading.

She had to give back most of the provisions and

thank-offerings the villagers had pressed on her, for she could not have used them up in a year's time, much less fit them all into her sledge. She bade the councillors good working and farewell, and told them to meet her upon the Open Hills beside the Plain of Providences that fall at reindeer time.

She went to Lasjmar next, the nearest village to Vlad and the second of the sixteen of her Tribe. Once more she was welcomed. After that, she went to Baslak and Insfélo, and each of the other lesser villages in turn. The task invigorated her, gave her a sense of urgency and purpose she had never known before.

Always, in every village, when she first arrived everyone came running and was curious, listening eagerly to her description of the *gristal* and the country beyond the Pole. But invariably when it came time to begin to build, some held back, watching still, and some shortly drifted away from the work. Others stood by, openly jeering.

When she questioned them, they often said, "We do not believe there is a land beyond the Plain of Broken Snow. All this effort will be for nothing."

"Then where do you think the reindeer go in winter?" she asked them.

At that they would shake their heads, still laughing. "We do not know, but it is no land where we may follow."

Others told her, "The world will not end. We do not believe in your Fireking. Your dreams are false."

"I have never said the world was ending," Caribou

replied. "It is changing. That is all that I have said."

Then sometimes they laughed again, or went away. Still others told her, "There is no escaping doom. Why try? If these firelords you speak of are angry with us, then we are meant to die." That puzzled her, for she had never told anyone that the firelords were angry.

They baffled her and troubled her, these people who would not join the work. She asked Reindeer one night about them when the two of them lay beside their campfire in the forest. The road between the village of Lukasj, which they had just departed, and Prino, where they were bound, was too long to travel — even by *gristal* — in a day.

Reindeer turned at her question to look at her, his golden eyes expressionless. "Why will they not build sledges — Cari, have you not asked them that yourself?"

She nodded, yawning, throwing another piece of deadwood on the fire. "Yes, but I find their answers very strange. Why will they not see the danger, and flee it while they can?"

She glanced at Reindeer and saw him gazing at her with the closest thing to amusement in his eyes that she had ever seen. But his tone was neutral still.

"Your people are indeed very strange," he said, "and have always puzzled me. But if even you, Cari, who are the wisest of them, do not understand them, how is it you hope that I, who am not even human, ever could?"

10

Tjaalsénji

THE LAST SETTLEMENT they went to was Tjaalsénji, the High City, where the chieftain of the
whole Tribe had lived before his death and where his
children still dwelled and quarreled. The village lay
in a high meadow that caught the morning sun. It
was late summer now, barely a month before the
autumnal equinox.

Caribou saw workers tilling the ripening fields as
she and Reindeer drew near, the landboat bucking and
sledding over the hard, slick road. Some of the workers looked up as she skimmed past, but none of them
paused from their tilling or pointed, shouting to their
companions, or dropped their tools and ran toward
her.

Instead, those that looked up turned back quickly
to their task, some going at it even more deter-
minedly. Caribou gazed at them, frowning. Never
before had she approached a town and not had people
cry out and run to meet her.

As they passed a woman weeding near the roadside,
Caribou reined in Reindeer.

"Is this the road to Tjaalsénji," she called, though
she did not doubt it, "and am I very far?"

The woman looked up, eyeing her resentfully, and answered curtly, "Yes and no," then turned back to her work.

Caribou stood a moment, not understanding, until she realized the woman had simply answered each of her questions in turn. She had shown no interest in the sledge.

"But —" Caribou began. The woman's head snapped up again, so swiftly that Caribou was startled. The field-worker's eyes were bright with loathing.

"Do not question me," she cried. "Vasli has told us of your coming. You are the false prophet from the Wildlands by the Waste, you with your talk of Firekings and your 'divine car' — divine indeed! — and your painted deer, spreading false rumors of the end of the world."

"He isn't —" Caribou started.

"*What?*" the woman shrieked.

"He isn't painted," Caribou repeated. This woman seemed almost a raver. The ties of her blouse were haphazardly looped, and dark circles curved beneath her eyes. "Gold is his own color," Caribou told her. "I have not gilded him."

"More lies," the woman spat. "Vasli has told us. You are in league with our foes. They set fire to the forests to blacken the sky, and shove rubble down the mountainsides to cause the earth to shake."

The woman had thrown down her spade and risen, wringing her hands. She glared at Caribou.

"Well, we are not frightened. Foes do not frighten us! You wish us to panic and lay ourselves open. Well, let others panic. Vasli protects us. What are a little smoke and trembling to us?"

She threw back her head then and gave a laugh, short and wild, then bit it off quickly and stared at Caribou.

"Who are these foes?" Caribou asked her, certain she could not mean the firelords. "The River-Valley People have fled away, and our villages are all one Tribe."

Reindeer was tugging at the reins, but Caribou held him.

"Renegades, then," the woman snapped, glancing off and shrugging frantically. "Or strangers. How should I know? I'm not Vasli. But Vasli has told us. Vasli says . . ."

"Who is Vasli?"

Reindeer stamped.

"Our leader!" The woman's eyes snapped back to Caribou. "The youngest, the only true son of Bhesjti, our late chief. Vasli knows — Vasli knows how things truly are."

Caribou studied the circles like berry-stains under the other's eyes. "How much sleep do you get . . . ?" she began.

"We *don't sleep*," the woman growled, snatching up her digging tool again. "We work — day and night. It is the only way we can keep ourselves ready."

Caribou stayed silent a moment. She glanced at Reindeer. He stood watching the woman digging. His golden eyes met Caribou's, but they told her nothing.

"Suppose I offered you an escape from this place,

these foes you fear," Caribou said to her. "Would you take it?"

"No!" the woman cried, spading furiously and tearing up the ripening crops as well as weeds now in her grubby fingers. "This is our land, *our* land. We will not leave it — not leave it, though the earth itself open and swallow us . . ."

Her words grew ragged, trailing off. Caribou saw the other's lips tremble, her breast heave and fall. Sweat or tears, Caribou could not tell which, made tracks along the woman's face. Her spade threw jets of soil into the air.

Caribou clucked to Reindeer and drove on.

The woman had been right; they were not far from the town. As they entered the outskirts, Caribou heard snatches of what sounded like singing — some near, some distant — and drunken revelry, though it was only late morning, and no feast-day.

Litter lay about the streets — broken drinking mugs, bread-heels, and half-picked bones. Household possessions lay strewn here and there, most dirtied or broken. The houses looked abandoned, many with a door or window staved in. More than once, in the distance, she heard shouts and the sound of splintering wood.

Three youths staggered out of an alleyway onto the main street ahead of her. One bore on his back a small chest and a sack. Another held an earthenware jug in each hand, and the third, a round of bread and a haunch of venison.

They were singing a drinking tune, but the words straggled off as they squinted and stared. Caribou and Reindeer glided by, but a little distance down the street Caribou pulled Reindeer to a halt, and turned to look at them over one shoulder.

"Ho, what says Vasli to this?" she cried. "Do not his followers hereabouts believe in work before there's war?"

The two youths with the chest and the bread blinked at her again, obviously baffled. But the other youth, the one with the wine jugs, who appeared younger and drunker than the other two, burst into laughter.

"Vasli?" he cried, hooted, almost unintelligible: "That no-name. *Vasli?* And war?" He roared. "There'll be no war. The world's about to end! And where . . . and just where . . . ?"

He staggered, trying to focus on her.

"May that . . . that is, may I . . ." He took a deep breath, got it sorted out. "And just where, may I ask, is it you've been this last twelvemonth, my young fine . . . fine young dame?"

His companions nudged him to silence then, eyeing her with some unease. They clearly took her for a person of importance. One of them hissed something at their companion. Caribou called to the other one, the one carrying bread and venison.

"Where may I find the town council?"

"Council hall's in the middle of town, Honor," the one she had addressed called. He seemed reluctant to approach. "Just follow the street."

"No councillors in it, though," the one with the

wine jugs called, over his companions' shushing. "All
gone — driven away. Council hall's gone, too. Burnt.
Brakla burnt it — all down."

"Who is Brakla?" Caribou asked.

The one with the chest and bag on his back bright-
ened. "Our leader, Worship," he called, beaming.
"Bhesjti's son."

Caribou nodded. "The only true child of the late
chieftain, I daresay."

"The truth!" the wine-jug lad cried with a hiccough
and a laugh. He had a dark, rather comely face, made
silly by drink. He reminded her vaguely of someone
she knew.

"And what does Brakla say?" Caribou inquired.

The one with the loaf and meat replied. "He says,
'be gay,' Honor! Be happy while you can. The world's
about to end. Why not? Eat, drink, live well — who
cares? None of it matters, and it's over too soon."

His companion with the wine jugs began a sort of
jig, accompanying himself with an off-key ditty, one
Caribou had not heard before:

> *"The end is near:*
> > *Soon falls the sky.*
> *I want to live*
> > *Before I die.*
>
> *So revel, feast —*
> > *Why let or stop?*
> *And foot the dance*
> > *Before we drop.*

> *Let mountains fall*
>   *And fountains churn.*
> *To sing's the thing*
>   *Before we burn . . . !"*

He lost his footing then and sprawled upon the cobbles, breaking one drinking jug with a crash. His companions snatched the other before he could do it damage. The one holding the chest set down his loot and began wrestling the fallen youth to his feet. The youth looked up at Caribou, still watching from a little distance.

"Join our . . . merry revel, Worship?" he managed.

Caribou turned to Reindeer and lifted the reins, let him draw her and their *gristal* away down the street.

As Caribou and Reindeer drew nearer to the center of town, the buildings began to look less disordered and deserted. Less rubbish lay about the streets. The houses were all shut tight.

As she neared the village square, she became aware of people, a long line, each group with a caribou calf that they were leading by the ear. Now and then, when the wind swung in the right direction, Caribou caught the scent of burning, and the sweet stench of the slaughterhouse. People turned to stare at her as she and Reindeer passed by.

When they reached the square, Caribou saw more villagers — though not really so many for such a great town as this. They were crowded about a great heap of ashes and charred timbers — the remains of the council hall, Caribou guessed.

As she got closer, she saw one knot of people with a caribou calf go forward. A tall woman wearing a white *mbolap* that fell to her knees and a headdress of caribou antlers stood upon the ashes, the fabric of her clothes spattered with wet red and drier brown. She held a long-bladed *ca'xat* in one hand.

The people brought the calf to the woman. She took it by the ear and cried out some garbled words toward the noon sky, which shone faint blue above the strands of gray smoke hanging in the air. Then she slashed the calf's throat with the blade. It fell struggling to the ash, and after a moment lay still. Two people, also in white, came forward and carried the carcass away as the woman carefully wiped the blade.

Caribou, shocked and alarmed, drew the sledge to a halt before the ashes of the council hall. The people there seemed to take note of her for the first time. They fell back, murmuring. The woman with the antlers looked up from her meticulous cleaning of the knife. She started, seeing Caribou, and her face, already hard, grew harder.

"Why have you come?" She lowered the blade, letting the white rag slip from her hand. "You who call yourself *i'dris* and wisewoman."

"I call myself neither," Caribou replied. Reindeer shook himself. The leather traces rattled and creaked.

"Why have you come?"

"I have come to offer safety to any who would have

it," Caribou answered, raising her voice enough for the others in the square to hear. "I come to warn you of the firelords' doing, how they are turning the earth to make it new again. I have come to show you how to build *gristaal,* that you may follow the reindeer with me beyond the Land of Broken Snow, and escape the changing of the earth."

"Go back," the woman in the horns spat. "We do not want you. We laugh at your firelords. You will die upon the Burning Plain if you try to follow the reindeer. I have heard of you and what you preach."

"I preach nothing," Caribou told her. "I am no godspeaker."

"All lies," the other shouted. "Emptiness and air!"

Caribou laid the reins of the sledge on the board in front of her and considered the woman across from her. "Since you already know my name," she said at last, "do me the kindness of telling me yours."

The other, in her bloodstained smock, drew herself up very straight. "I am Nilsa, first and only daughter of Bhesjti. I wear the horns of leadership now."

Caribou eyed her, and wondered that the people of the square stood so quiet, so lifeless, so cowed. "You have two brothers, so I have heard, who say similarly," she observed.

"I spit on those mice!" the antlered woman shouted, clutching her knife. "*I* am the eldest-born. It is I who am best-suited to lead the Tribe." She gestured, smiling now. "And, as you see, the people follow me. Not them — or you."

Caribou glanced around her, dismayed, at the silent, meager crowd in the square. "Why are you slaughtering your caribou calves?"

"Hah!" the eldest-born of Bhesjti cried. "Wise-woman indeed — you fraud. We sacrifice them to the ancestors. The daimons, too, are angry with us. We had forgotten them and turned away. They shake the ground and boil the blood of the earth to remind us how we have failed them with our faithlessness."

"The *waijen* live across the sky in the Land of Endless Night," said Caribou, "and the daimons have all gone away. What good does the blood of caribou do such as they?"

The other woman shouted with laughter, but the crowd about them remained motionless, quiet. "Why, it satisfies them, propitiates them. They drink it up" — she gestured — "like wine."

"The earth drinks it," Caribou told her, "and trembles still."

The antlered woman did not reply, but nodded curtly, right and left. A knot of white-robed assistants on either side of her started forward. Caribou felt a surge of alarm.

"Enough of these words," the daughter of Bhesjti hissed. A little smile twisted her lips. "Let us see how the gods like the blood of your painted deer — or *your* blood, seeing-woman, if it comes to that."

Reindeer snorted, wheeling in the traces. Caribou hastily gathered the reins and held him back. He would have fallen on Nilsa's henchmen if she had let him. Reindeer struck the cobbles with his hooves and danced. The assistants halted in confusion. Some of them held cudgels of black, charred wood. Nilsa stood furious, with folded arms.

Reindeer did not fight Caribou as she turned him, but sprang away, drawing the sledge behind him in a swift, smooth sweep. She circled the square once, crying to the people who yet stood still, like stone, holding their caribou calves and watching her with dull, hopeless eyes.

"Any of you who would follow me, any of you who would learn to build a landboat such as this one and escape with me across the Burning Plain, come now, come soon, to the nearby villages: Fusklaf, or Kiord, or Ersk. They are building sledges there and will welcome you."

Behind her, she heard Nilsa speaking harshly to her servants, urging them after the sledge. Caribou kept Reindeer moving in a wide arc, and cried out once more to the people in the square.

"But if you stay here past our departure in the autumn, when the reindeer are running, surely you will all perish, for the firelords here are changing the earth, like a *trangl* throwing its skin — without a thought that mortal creatures such as we may not survive the flash. Come away with me and save yourselves!"

The sparse crowd neither moved nor spoke. She glimpsed the assistants of the chieftain's daughter following her now, trotting half-heartedly after the sledge. Reindeer completed his circuit of the square and sprang off down the side-street by which he and she had come.

Glancing back, Caribou spotted the assistants standing at the square's edge, gazing after her now less with anger than with apathy. Again she heard their leader crying out, her words unintelligible. Caribou shuddered and clapped the reins for more speed from her golden Reindeer, so eager was she to be gone from that place.

11

The Plain of Providences

AFTER the High City of Tjaalsénji, Reindeer and
Caribou returned home. They spent the last
days of summer laying in their provisions and awaiting the cooler weather that would bring the wild deer.
When the time arrived, in the midst of fall, Reindeer
came to her in his man-shape as she sat upon the
hearth, brewing berries into sweet jam.

"Cari," he told her, "the reindeer are running. I
feel it. My blood flows quicker with their running,
and I am restless. Their snorting and stamping and
their wild cries call me."

Caribou nodded without looking up and laid down
the sticky spoon with which she ladled off the dross.

"I know it," she answered. "I dreamed of it last
night."

And the golden arrow had turned very strongly in
her hand this morning, when she had held it, as it
always did when the wild herd was near. Reindeer
sat beside her at the hearth's edge. She sighed.

"We must pack the sledge tomorrow," she said,
"and shut up the house. You must throw on your
reindeer skin again and don the traces. Then we will
go down the Open Hills, where they meet the Plain

of Providences, which the wild deer must cross to reach their Path which funnels them on to the Burning Plain. There we will meet those who would come with us to the world's other side, and await the reindeer."

He nodded, still not speaking, seeming at once both restive and weary. Caribou poured the hot, bubbling jam, smelling of mint and stewed berries, into earthen pots, and melted wax over them to seal the lids. Then she laid them along the wall in the coldest part of the lodge.

Reindeer meanwhile went to their bed and threw off his man-clothes. He crawled beneath the fur of the golden deer-pelt. Caribou came back to the hearth but did not bank the fire. He watched her for a little while, sleepy-seeming, and held out his hand to her at last.

"Are you not coming?"

"You sleep," she bade him, rising and going to lift the lid of the chest where she stored her birks and needles. "I will come in a little while."

The next morning they rose before first light and laid all the stores they would need in the hold of the sledge: dried meat and bread, preserves of fruit and fat bitternuts, fish roe in pots and honey, soap and tallow candles, oil for burning, tinder, wicks, and many kinds of tools, all wrapped in woven cloth and furs, wedged tight and laced firmly down.

It was still the earliest part of the day, just past dawn, when they finished. Reindeer came to where she stood in her travel furs, and asked, "Where are the traces? I cannot find them. How shall I pull the sledge without them — have you seen them? Did you bring them into the house last night?"

Caribou went into the dark, shut-up *ntula* for the last time and opened the chest where she had kept her birks and sewing things. She brought out the tack and harness she had laid there the evening before and carried them out to Reindeer, jingling and tinkling like a thousand bits of glass.

"Bells," he cried, astonished, fingering them. "You have sewn them all with bells."

She nodded. "Last night, while you slept. It came to me that our sledge might well be lost from sight at times, hidden by fog or smoke. These bells will sound above the clack and thunder of the wild deer's running, and our followers will know where we are."

He ran his hands over the traces then, examining the bells. "You carved these of my father's bones."

Again, her nod. "A long time past, when first you went away. I did not know why at the time. I forgot about them afterward, till now."

Reindeer dropped the traces suddenly, took her face in his hands. He cradled it a moment, then bent and kissed her. She clung to him and did not want to let him go. But he drew away from her, gently, and threw off the man-clothes she had made for him. He donned the golden reindeer pelt, skin-side to his skin.

Caribou hid her eyes from the brilliant light. She told herself she must not weep. *He is not really leaving me. The transformation is necessary. He must be a stag for a little while now, so that he may pull the sledge.* But that did not ease the ache in her heart. Already she was longing for him in his man-shape again — but when she looked up, her fair-skinned youth was a deer again, just shrugging into the belled traces.

Sighing, she buckled them, then took the reins and climbed into the driver's box, dropping the bar across the open space behind her so that she might lean back against it if she liked. Then she clucked to Reindeer and let him take her — bounding and leaping as though the sledge's weight were nothing to him, his tendons snapping and the harness singing — away toward their meeting with the others of her Tribe.

From the hilly Wilds that bordered on the Broken Plain, they came down and inland toward the rolling, treeless tableland her people called the Open Hills. The sky hung lower now, gray with clouds and smoke. The Spouting Springs, a low range of geysers off to the west, were breathing cinders and steam. From time to time, as she and Reindeer drew near the flatter tundra called the Plain of Providences, Caribou heard the distant crash of geysers splitting rock.

They came upon the others almost before she was aware, nearly stumbling into the midst of their encampment before the ragged veil of fog parted, revealing them. Reindeer snorted, and Caribou reined in. The jingling of his bells abruptly ceased.

She stared at the group of sledges before her. Teams of four and six caribou lounged in their traces. Off to one side, a common herd milled about a makeshift enclosure of sledges and campfires. Caribou looked around in dismay. The people standing among the sledges stared back at her.

"Is this all," she cried at last, "all that came?" The meager crowd before her would scarcely have peopled two of the sixteen villages of the Tribe. Caribou glanced about. "Or are the others late?"

Reindeer shook himself. The bells whirred and jingled like cricket-song. The people before her were shaking their heads. She recognized a face, one of the elders who had come to her in spring.

"No more than this, *i'dris,*" the woman said, her worn fingers playing with the beads in one braid. "They laughed us out of town in most of our villages, for many have turned away from the work and against you since you came. Though the daimons are gone and the charms no longer work, though the earth trembles still, most no longer take heed." She bowed her head. "No more are coming, *i'dris.*"

Caribou shook her head, appalled, for the tremors of the earth and the black cinder-clouds had grown even more frequent, more violent since spring. Reindeer stood in the traces before her, golden and unperturbed. Her mouth felt dry.

"The councillors," she said at length. "How many of them came?"

She spotted others now, moving among the crowd. Her voice carried well over the open, rolling hills. The ragged fog had begun to lift; a faint breeze fanned her cheek. She saw the councilwoman glancing at the others.

"All of us," she said, and other voices echoed, "All of us came, *i'dris*."

Caribou's heart grew warmer then. For the first time she was able to smile. At least the elders had not lost faith in her. She sighed. It was too late to do anything about the rest. The people before her stood waiting, expectant.

"Well, so be it," said Caribou. "If this is our number, we must be content."

She felt her blood beginning to quicken. From far in the northern distance, coming over the Plain from beyond the horizon's edge, she could hear the reindeer running. She did not see them yet, but they made the ground tremble even here, even so far.

The caribou were growing restless in their pen. Reindeer stamped one hoof and champed. Others of her people had caught sound of the thunder now. She saw them turning their heads, scanning — and then the vast wild herd hove into sight over the rim of the world. They closed rapidly, until soon the ground was trembling so violently that Caribou half believed the rumble must be the earth itself, and not the wild deer.

From their vantage point on the last of the hills, she and her people watched the tide of silver thundering past. Far ahead, to the south, where the tundra rose to meet the Wilderlands, they could see the living river narrow, bunching as the reindeer reached the glacier-trough and plunged into its bottleneck, which channeled them toward the Land of Broken Snow.

The caribou within the enclosure circled restively,

while those in the traces strained and bawled so the people could scarcely hold them. Caribou kept her arm raised to keep her people back — the golden arrow held in one hand — for she dared not let them brave that headlong, trampling rush.

At last the great flood had swept by them and, as if at some unspoken signal, the caribou in the enclosure stampeded, leaping the barricades to follow. "Let them go; let them go," Caribou cried to those trying frantically to re-corral them. "It is time we were away ourselves."

She let her hand fall forward, southward, pointing.

"Let us run across the Land of Broken Snow," she shouted, "chasing the wild deer — to the Pole, and beyond, to the other side of the world."

Reindeer sprang away at Caribou's word. With a shout, the others scrambled to their sledges, the drivers leaping onto the back-end step, passengers bundling themselves onto the baggage hold in front and lapping their furs.

Caribou saw all this in a rush as Reindeer bounded away, dragging her sledge more easily and swiftly than the teams of four and six caribou behind them pulled theirs. The bells settled themselves into a chanting rhythm in time with Reindeer's pacing stride. Glancing back, she saw the rest fanning out behind, their draft-caribou beginning to find their strides and the last few unhitched caribou running alongside and among them.

They ran until they neared the tundra's edge, where

the ground rose and funneled into the glacier trough. Caribou could see the dark, moving mass that was the last of the reindeer passing into the funnel ahead, and heard their distant thunder, more faintly now, above the clacking of her own Tribe's caribou and the singing of Reindeer's bells.

As they drew near the tundra's narrowing, near the low, wooded slopes that formed the northern extreme of the Wilderlands through which the funnel traveled, Caribou suddenly spotted people — Tribeswomen, and men, a few children — most of them ragged and exhausted, standing among the trees.

A few staggered down the short hillside toward the sledges. Caribou had swept past the first of them almost before she saw them. They held out their hands to the passing *gristaal*. Caribou could hear some of their cries.

"Help us!" someone shouted. "Take us with you!"

"The mountain," another voice, a woman's, called. "The mountain by Aba Barkán has fallen. We saw it from across the valley at Davín — all firefall and killing smoke. We ran, but most could not escape."

"It is the end of the world!" an old woman screamed.

"Take us with you; take us with you, *i'dris*," Caribou heard someone pleading. "You were right. Oh, save us. We must get away!"

Caribou tried to slow Reindeer then, but he had taken the bit in his teeth. He ran on faster than before. Caribou shouted for him to stop, and when he would not, she turned to call back over her shoulder to the others in sledges behind her, "Have you room to take some of these people with you?"

Those on the landboats shook their heads. One of them, a man with two children on a heavily burdened *gristal,* cried back, "We've neither space nor weight to spare, *i'dris.* We are loaded as much as may be."

Another man called out; Caribou thought she recognized him as one of the council members. "We cannot take on any more load without killing our caribou or falling behind — and if we lose the reindeer, how will we find our way across the Burning Plain?"

Caribou tugged at the useless reins. The ground shuddered suddenly underfoot; the sledge lurched. Caribou pitched painfully against the rail. She heard a roar like shifting earth, saw those on foot by the hillside stagger.

She heard the wild snorts and whistles of frightened caribou. Reindeer sprang into a faster lope. Behind her, more people came running over the crest of the hill. Smoke billowed up from beyond the trees.

"The geyser has flung itself apart!" a fleeing woman cried. "The earth has split and is spouting fire. The woods are burning! The woods —"

Screaming followed and shouts of dismay from those driving the sledges. People on foot fled the hillside, dashing onto the plain. The earth shuddered again with a terrible groaning. Caribou clung to the rail of her *gristal,* and this time she saw spouts of fire beyond the crest of the wooded hill. Smoke roiled up. Before her and behind, people rushed for the landboats, seized hold of the sides, tried to drag out their occupants.

Caribou heard curses, shouting, moans, and prayers from both the sledge-drivers and those grappling with them. The free caribou dashed wildly among the *gristaal* now. Some of the people who had rushed to the sledges managed to cling for a few moments, only to fall at last — sometimes beneath some caribou's heels. Caribou watched, horrified and helpless.

Someone, a youth, seized hold of the side of her *gristal* suddenly. He clutched her arm, and she tried to pull him up, but he fought her clumsily — and she realized, astonished, that he was trying to fling her from the landboat. Terror surged in her. She fended him off. Gritting her teeth, she kicked him hard in the chest. He fell. She clung to the rail of the *gristal,* gasping, and did not look behind.

Up ahead she saw Reindeer lower his horns and toss aside a man who had planted himself squarely in their path, his *ca'xat* drawn. Caribou bit back a cry. She fumbled with the dangling reins and managed to catch hold of them, lift them up so they could not tangle Reindeer's heels.

The ground shuddered for a third time, most violently. She saw the surface of the tundra pull apart like rent cloth. In places the cracks were an el across. Reindeer vaulted over these, and the sledge bucked roughly. The people on foot were falling behind them now. The sledges had all swept past. Caribou saw bodies lying scattered on the cracked tundra.

Sparks of fire gusted over the hillcrest. Flames appeared in the crowns of the trees; more cries came from those who fled on foot behind, curses and wails of despair. Smoke billowed down as the wind whipped over the hill. Some of it smelled like burning pine, and the rest like poison stench. Caribou held a flap of her *lanlan* over her face.

"More speed!" she cried. "We must get past. There is death in this smoke — it comes of burning rock!"

The drivers following her whipped their caribou into a hurtling run. Though swifter than all of them, Reindeer was keeping his pace in check so as not to outdistance the others. His bells chanted above the sound of caribou hooves, clacking tendons, sliding runners, and the commotion of forest and earth behind.

The unharnessed caribou had begun to outstrip the sledges now. Reindeer let them pull past him and run on ahead after the wild deer. Moments later, Caribou started as the walls of a canyon loomed suddenly and swallowed them. *The glacier-trough.*

They were running the Path of the reindeer now, tracing their passage through the Wilderland. Caribou cast her eyes behind her one last time, but what little she could see through the canyon's mouth was a dismal haze of fire and smoke.

12

The Land of
Broken Snow

THEY RAN and twisted, sledding through the great
glacier-trough, following their own deer as they
chased the even greater thunder of the wild deer, invisible now beyond the closer caribou.

Gazing back, Caribou saw the other sledges bunched
in the turning meanders of the trough. The ground
was shaking under the sledge-runners from the reindeer's passing. Caribou rested the reins on the rail and
let Reindeer run as he pleased.

Sometime later they neared the end of the narrow
gorge. Caribou glimpsed ahead of them the last of the
reindeer, fanning out over the snowy plain like a gray
torrent. The caribou, like a much smaller rivulet, did
the same, spreading and running southward after the
wild deer.

Caribou reined her golden stag in a little as they
left the canyon's steep, high walls behind, looked back
over her shoulder at their little band. She circled as
the last of them emerged from the canyon, raising her
golden arrow high.

"Follow," she cried. "The reindeer run far ahead
of us now. Quickly! We must catch them."

Reindeer wheeled, sped off across the Broken Plain,

and Caribou let him run for a few moments before pulling back gently to remind him that the others had not his speed. Her *trangl* dropped to a rapid trot; his belled harness chanted and sang.

The ground over which they sledded now was hard and hot. Caribou felt its warmth rising moist against her unmuffled face. Some places seemed warmer than others, though, and she saw great swatches where snow had formed, interspersed with patches of exposed, sometimes steaming ground.

The vast herd ahead of them had trampled down much of the snow, but here and there whole stretches lay undisturbed. Reindeer, too, refused to tread them, even when Caribou tried guiding him toward one. He only clamped the bit more firmly in his teeth and tossed his head from side to side.

Not long after, she realized that some of the sledges forming the leading edge of the fan had begun to pull ahead of her. They were driven by maidens and youths mostly, lashing their teams to greater speed, laughing and racing. Caribou only glanced at them at first, shaking her head. She decided to let them run a bit till their hot heads cooled.

"Snow!" she heard one of the young women call out suddenly. "Fresh snow!"

Another voice took up the cry.

Then, "A race! Come, Val, Tor. We'll race!"

Looking ahead, Caribou saw the snow — a broad, soft expanse of white, unusually deep, perhaps knee-high. At the same moment she felt a change in Reindeer's stride.

Three sledges were veering toward the snow blanket, the drivers tapping their caribou into a gallop with their willow flicks. They cut across Caribou's path, laughing and shouting, ignoring the cries of their elders. Caribou shouted a warning, too, but they only lashed their teams and swept by.

Caribou gathered in the reins, but before she could so much as clap them, Reindeer had sprung into a gallop on his own. Their sledge bolted in pursuit, passing two of the three *gristaal* in a moment.

Reindeer gave a bell-like cry. The caribou teams of those two sledges flicked their ears to the sound, then wheeled, galloping back to rejoin the others despite their drivers' dismayed and angry cries.

The third sledge had a much greater lead and was by this time almost to the snow. Reindeer redoubled his speed, but just as he drew even with it, that sledge's team vaulted up onto the snowbed. The landboat bucked up behind — they were running along the snow's edge now, Caribou and Reindeer along the flat.

"Hah!" cried the youth at the reins of the other *gristal,* "so you'd race with us, wisewoman? Let us see if six earthly caribou can outrun your golden stag!"

He lashed his team with his long willow wand and his landboat leapt ahead. For a moment, Caribou could only stare, for she had recognized him — one of the three youths she had seen in Tjaalsénji, the one who had been carrying the chest. Were those his two companions on the sledge with him?

Caribou shoved useless wondering away and clapped

the reins to Reindeer, but he was already lengthening his stride. Pulling even again with the sledge on the snow, he gave a long, belling cry, and the caribou in the other teams faltered, falling back. Their driver leaned forward and lashed them again.

"Ho, no magic from your golden deer, wise-woman," he cried. "Let the race be fair!"

One of his companions urged him on. Caribou could see them better now, and recognized them both. The younger, darker one did not join in the hying. He seemed sober enough now, a little pale, and not half so exhilarated as his fellows. For a moment, his eyes met Caribou's.

"Rein in, you fool," she cried at the driver. "This is treacherous ground. Why do you think the reindeer have not —"

The phrase died on her lips as, abruptly, she felt Reindeer shorten his stride. Glancing ahead, she saw where the snow blanket suddenly widened. If the two sledges held course, both would be up on the snow soon, and in the middle of it, no longer on the edge.

Reindeer bolted forward, and Caribou had to clutch the rail to keep from falling. Her golden stag drew ahead of the other sledge till Caribou herself was opposite the lead team. Then Reindeer veered hard toward the team, within an arm's length of them.

Caribou stood mystified. Why did Reindeer not turn, away from the snow? They would be on it themselves in another minute if they did not veer. Reindeer gave out a long, bawling cry. The caribou of the other team lifted their heads, swerving toward Caribou.

The other driver lashed and cursed his team, fighting to pull them away, but the caribou strained toward her still, leaning out their necks — and all at once she understood. Dropping her own reins, she reached as far as she could across the rail to grasp the cheek strap of the nearest caribou. They were almost to the snow.

"I have it," she shouted. "Reindeer, I have it in hand!"

With a cry, the golden stag shied, very hard. Caribou was thrown to her knees on the driver's step, but she clung tight to the rail and managed to keep her grip on the team's bridle. Then the caribou came down off the snow, and the violence of their descent jerked the cheek strap from her hand.

She saw the other *gristal,* still on the snow, break through a sort of crust underneath. The rear half of the sledge's near runner fell through with a muffled crunch. The whole landboat tilted. Driver and passengers cried out, clung to the sledge. Thick, gray water spattered up, and Caribou heard shouts of pain, surprise, as droplets touched faces and hands.

The caribou struggled forward, bawling. Caribou managed to get hold again, this time of the strap linking the bits of the lead pair. She braced herself. The sledge behind her came free of the snowbank, crashing down on the hard ground — and the runners held.

Caribou let go of the strap. Shaking, she got to her feet. Her chest above the breasts felt bruised where it had met the rail, and her fingers and knees were gashed. Panting, trying to regain her breath, she caught up the dangling reins of the six-caribou sledge and led it back to rejoin the others. Neither the young driver nor his passengers protested now, but instead sat clinging to their *gristal*.

Caribou flung them their reins, then circled the other sledges to shout: "This is the Burning Plain, the Land of Broken Snow. There is fire in the earth here, and hidden pools of caustic water. Who dare forget that now? Run only where the reindeer have run, and follow my golden stag. Only he has run this path before. Only he can lead the way."

She let Reindeer take her to the front of the band then, drawing out well ahead so that all might see her, yet still hear the chanting of his bells.

They ran on, beneath a hidden sun that skulked behind the high, gray clouds. The reindeer had become no more than a dark mass on the far horizon, and the caribou were only a little less far ahead. They ran past places where rocks littered the ground. They skated vast flats where the earth was cracked and level.

For long stretches they passed over only trampled snow. The going was smoother there, and at such times Caribou felt both herself and her people grow easier. Other times they wove through great fields of shallow water, patched with algae and mineral scum, dull gray, reflecting the duller sky.

Sometimes, when the ground was hard and hot, the heat rose so intensely that Caribou felt her armpits growing slick and had to open the throat and sleeves of her *lanlan* to let in enough wind to cool her.

Time passed. The sun, hidden behind the clouds, declined, and the afternoon grew late. Often when the terrain ahead looked regular and safe, Caribou circled back to survey her band. Their going had grown much slower now.

Though she trusted that they had been training their teams to run long stretches without tiring as she had bade them, she could see that the caribou were finding the pace hard going. They could barely keep up a ragged trot. And with the unharnessed caribou now far ahead, there would be no changing spent animals for fresh.

The people themselves looked weary and dispirited. They no longer shouted and called to one another as they drove, or laughed with giddy release at the dizzying speed. They talked to her sometimes, as she circled them, working her way back up through their ranks.

"*I'dris,* when will we get there?" a young girl cried, and then her brother, even younger, yawning, echoed, "Aren't we there yet, wisewoman?"

"*I'dris,* I'm so hungry. Can't we stop and eat?"

"I have to rest! I'm so tired I can hardly stand."

"The trace-caribou, *i'dris,* look at them. They're staggering."

"It's so hot here, it's like a spring."

"Take heart," called Caribou. "I cannot say how long we must run, for the wild deer run this trek without resting, and we must do the best we can. If you are hungry, eat of your stores. Have you not kept them close at hand as I instructed you? If you are warm, unlatch your *lanlani*. If you are tired, those of you who are not minding the reins pillow your heads and sleep. The Burning Plain cannot last forever. When we are past it, we will stop."

Caribou clucked to her golden stag and let Reindeer take her up to the head of the band. Dusk fell, grayly; it hung a long time in the sky. The air grew cooler, though gusts of steam still rose from the warm, flat earth.

The character of the land had begun to change — it was still flat where they traveled now, but the horizon ahead seemed elevated, uneven, like a low ridge of hills. Then Caribou discovered with a start that she could no longer see the dark tide of reindeer before them. It was only the smaller, lighter band of caribou that she could make out, far on the limit of her vision.

As she watched, she saw them, too, beginning to dwindle and disappear over the horizon's rim. Her skin grew cold, and her heart sank like a stone. Her dreams had not shown her any of this — nor indeed anything of what lay beyond the Plain of Providences, she realized. She had come on Reindeer's word alone, with blind trust in him and in his tales of sweet pastures beyond the snows.

A momentary panic gripped her. *Should I have placed my faith in a daimon?* she wondered. *What do I really know of him now, of what he has become? Does he love me — does he truly care what happens to my people, or is he just using me, using us all somehow, for some unfathomable purpose of his own?*

She fought the icy terror down. *No. I trust Reindeer;*

I must *trust him. For he loves me. He must.* But she shivered still. She had no more definite idea of where they were going, of how to get there, or of how long they must go than the people who followed her.

Night settled, deepening from pale gray through charcoal toward black. When there was yet the barest trace of light left to see by, Caribou reined gently, and Reindeer slowed, coming at last to a stop.

She had felt the land beginning to change again beneath the sledge's runners, growing hillier and cooler. Though she wanted to get beyond the worst of the Burning Plain before halting, now she feared to leave it entirely and so lose its warmth.

She stepped down from the halted sledge, feeling the slight heat rising through the soles of her boots, and managed a smile. She had gauged it right. Though warm, the ground here was cool enough to camp upon. She waved and shouted to the others. The dozing drivers gliding past her jerked awake, reining in their teams. Exhausted caribou collapsed in their traces.

With the cessation of the bells and the cracking of caribou tendons, with no more dull thud of hooves or hissing grind of runners on the hard earth, all the world seemed suddenly, oddly, utterly still. Caribou stood beside Reindeer and gazed at the tired people around them, stumbling down from their sledges.

"Let lamps be lit," she told them, "and fires made. Prepare food and skins for sleeping. Tend your caribou. We will travel again at first light."

The people turned and followed her instructions —

numbly, like sleepwalkers. Fires were struck up. She saw food and bedding being unpacked. No one answered her. No one spoke to anyone else. Their silence niggled at her, like an itch between the shoulder blades, but she shook it off. *I am weary myself,* she thought. She unharnessed Reindeer and walked with him through the silent others to the edge of the camp.

She could see little of their surroundings for the dark, but the terrain was more hilly now than it had been. Lichens and reindeer moss crunched with the pebbles underfoot. She stood with her golden stag beyond the light of the nearest fire. They both stared toward the midnight Pole.

"Reindeer, do you know where we are?" she asked him quietly.

The gold deer snorted and lifted his head. Pensive, she fingered the thick, golden hairs of his hide, frustrated that he could not throw off his deer-shape even for a little — but there was no cover here to conceal the brilliance of the light his transformation always made, and he was shy of people. She remembered his words from before their departure: *The route changes a little every year as the Burning Plain shifts itself and changes.*

"What lies ahead —" she began again, and was startled at the sound of her own voice in the stillness. She dropped it to a murmur: "the Fount of Gold?"

The *trangl* bowed his head and stamped.

She sighed, resting her head against him a moment. "Aye, that and more, I suppose."

She gazed at the last of the dusklight abandoning

the sky, and was aware for the first time of a dim glow in the south, red above the low, near hills. She had thought all this while that it was some reflection of the smoldering sun, but she saw now that it could not be, must be instead the reflection of some other, reddish light beyond the horizon's edge.

"What is it?" she asked Reindeer. "Do you know?"

She felt the golden stag tense beneath her hand. Again he snorted, stamped. She could not tell whether he meant that as an affirmation or denial.

"Can you tell me?"

He shook his head, great gold eyes gazing into hers with no expression. She held his head in her hands and gazed in return. Her voice was more hushed when at last she spoke. Her dreams had told her nothing of this.

"It is something wondrous," she asked him, "is it not? And terrible."

But his deer's eyes could not answer her. He leaned forward and touched his nose to her cheek, then pulled away. He was leaving her. She sensed it suddenly and struggled to be calm.

"Will you go and scout the way for us?" she asked.

The stag half turned, eyeing her over one shoulder. Her voice rose.

"Will you be back by morning?"

Her *trangl* bowed his head, then leapt away into the dark. With a little cry, Caribou reached after him, but he was already gone. Unbidden tears sprang to her eyes, but she shook her head angrily and brushed them away. *I am behaving like a frightened child,* she told herself. *He will return. Of course he will.* She sighed and worked her shoulders then. Her body felt knotted with fatigue. She stared into the dark a little while longer, then at last turned wearily and started back toward the camp.

13

Tor

CARIBOU NOTICED that the people had grouped their burning oil-pots into rings and drawn their teams and sledges into rough circles around their fires — more for light and companionship, she guessed, than for warmth. The night was not yet truly cold. Still no one spoke as she passed, though now it seemed that quiet conversations broke off at her approach, and the people watched her.

She found that a circle of oil-pots had formed alongside her *gristal*. Caribou unpacked her own oil-pot, placing it among the rest, and set a bowl of frozen lard and rabbit's meat over the flame, as others had done, to thaw the meat.

Some of the faces around the fire she recognized. Three of them were members of the embassy that had come to her in spring. She glanced at Djenret of Vlad, but he quickly looked down and seemed uncomfortable. There was little speaking, and all of that in low murmurs. The food in the pots bubbled, giving off savory smells.

Caribou lifted her coal-hot bowl from the flame with a rabbitskin, set it in its muffler, and ate. Others about the campfire were doing the same. With the warmth of food in her, a little of her weariness left her, but still no one spoke, and the silence weighed on her.

At last Djenret, sitting across from her, laid down his bowl. Caribou heard others in the ring draw breath, their eyes darting between her and the councilman. Uneasily, Caribou laid down her own dish. She felt those around other fire-rings turning to watch as well.

"Wisewoman," the gray-haired elder began, gazing at his lined and craggy hands, and not at her. "It has been decided . . . That is, we have discussed among ourselves . . ."

Words failed him. He groped, still looking down — at the firepots now. Then he glanced up, his eyes barely brushing hers before springing away.

"While you stood with your reindeer at camp's edge," the councilman told her, "some people came to me, a number of people — many of us. And we fear . . ."

He glanced at her again, but Caribou would not help him. The unease in her had grown very sharp. She said nothing, moved not at all, only waited.

"*I'dris,* we fear that we are lost."

Caribou's eyes widened. She drew breath in surprise, but the councilman hurried on.

"Wisewoman, we have lost the reindeer — can you deny it? Brikka and many others saw them disappearing over the horizon's edge before dusk — our caribou as well."

Caribou clenched her teeth against the bitter taste that had come into her mouth. She kept her voice steady. "Aye."

The councilman looked up, his own frustration clear. "Well, how shall we catch them, then? You told us we must run behind the reindeer, but the reindeer run without resting — and our caribou seem to have done the same."

"They have stolen our caribou," she heard an old woman from another circle cry. "The wild deer have."

The councilman said, "Without our herds, we cannot change our sledge-teams. And we ourselves must stop to rest as well. How will we ever find the wild deer now? We are lost."

Caribou folded her arms across her drawn-up knees, for she was cold. Djenret of Vlad spoke more truth than she would have wished — all except for that last. They had indeed lost their own herd and the wild deer. She had not anticipated that — nor, she guessed, had Reindeer.

But she refused to believe they were lost, not while her *trangl* was with them. Despite her alarm when she had seen the caribou vanish, and again when Reindeer had bounded away into the dark, Caribou gritted her teeth against despair and answered Djenret and the others as openly and encouragingly as she could.

"The wild deer we will never catch, but our caribou we will find awaiting us when we have reached the other side of the world. I am certain of it."

"And when will that be?" she heard a man's voice demand. She fought the urge to snap back at him.

"Who can say?" she replied evenly. "Only the reindeer have run this path before, and they run without resting, as we cannot. We must simply go on, as long as we must, until we are there."

"But we are so tired!" someone cried.

"And what lies ahead of us?" exclaimed a woman in Caribou's own circle. "Exhaustion and hunger — more hardship and pain? The earth here is strange and treacherous, worse than our homeland. We may all die . . ."

Her last words were drowned out by some man's angry shout: "And what is that red glow in the sky to the south of us? Answer us that."

Murmurs and cries of approval followed — angry, cutting. Their ugliness astonished her. Caribou was on her feet before she knew it. The blood came to her face, though her body still shivered and felt cold. Her hands clenched into fists, but with an effort, she held herself in check. She answered the man behind her without turning; her words were for them all.

"You speak of the red glow ahead. But how many of you have heeded that even fiercer glow to the north, whence we came?"

She pointed, hardly looking herself, felt people all around her turning. She heard gasps, and murmurs of fear.

"Two things only make such a glow," she told them, "Brimming rock spilling from the earth and forests rabid with fire. Do you wish to return, to that?"

She fell silent a moment and let them think. She

looked at Djenret. The councilman sat tugging nervously on his moustache. Then she looked at each one of her own ring in turn before casting her voice out onto the stillness again for all to hear.

"One thing is certain: we cannot go back. Our homes are no more! The firelords have awakened the earth. Already it is changing its skin. Nothing remains of what we left behind. Have you forgotten the terror in which you sent your embassy to me last spring? 'Save us from the quaking of the earth and the fountains of fire, O *i'dris!*' "

She stood, breathing hard. Anger made her breathless.

"You call me wisewoman. Do you think then that I am not wise? That I do not, now and again, dream dreams that speak the truth?"

She pierced them once again with her gaze, and fought to be calm. Where was Reindeer? She wanted him. Why had he not stayed with her — why had she let him go? But she had no time for useless thoughts, and shoved them angrily away. Facing her people, she made her voice sure and strong.

"How many of you have I helped through my judgments and dreams? And I tell you now that not long after your council came to me, I dreamed a dream that spoke of burning brush and running firestone, streaming sea and a moon of blood. I would not have dreamed these things if they were not to come to pass. Which of you would go home now?"

Silence greeted her. No one spoke, though there were murmurs, mutters, and shifting glances among

the people. Caribou eyed the councilman across from
her and the woman who had cried out. Neither of
them would look at her.

Someone spoke. "But we are lost, *i'dris.*" It was a
boy's voice, afraid. "The reindeer have run away."

Caribou sighed, letting some of the fierceness fade
from her. "We will not see them again," she replied,
more gently now, "until we have reached the land we
seek, but we can follow their footsteps."

"And where the ground is hard, where there is no
snow?" A woman's voice.

"Where no tracks show, my golden Reindeer will
lead us," said Caribou. "He knows the way."

"Your golden reindeer has deserted you," she heard
another woman crying out. The accusation cut her to
the bone, but Caribou only shook her head.

"He will return by morning. He has but gone to
scout the way."

"Lies!" the same voice replied. "Nilsa was right. I
should have stayed in Tjaalsénji! You are a false
prophetess . . ."

The nails of Caribou's fingers bit into her palms.
She wanted to fly at the follower of Nilsa and scratch
her eyes. She wanted to weep. Reindeer, Reindeer —
where was Reindeer? She held herself back.

"You have led us here but to leave us to die," a
man was saying.

"That is not so!" answered Caribou, with such force
that she cut the other short.

"Then perhaps, *i'dris,* you are misled," the councilman's voice began, "your reindeer false . . ."

"Nor is that so," spat Caribou, taking a step toward Djenret. She stopped herself, unclenched her fists, and drew deep breaths, remembering Reindeer's words to her once, when he had been a child.

Cari, your sudden fits of anger or of tears startle me and serve no purpose that I can see.

She made herself outwardly calm. Carefully, she reached behind her and lifted her golden arrow from where it lay close at hand on her sledge. She held it up so that it glinted in the yellow oil-light.

"But even were that so," she said, pitching her voice to carry, but less angry now, "even were it so that my Reindeer had left me, it would make no matter. This arrow that I carry points ever toward the wild deer, wherever they may be."

She threw the arrow down. It fell within the ring of oil-pots of her own circle. The arrow lay golden upon the ground, pointing due south. The crowd was silent.

"And the runners of my sledge," said Caribou, "are shod with the self-same gold."

Djenret was leaning forward between the flaring oil-pots. He held a stick in his hand. Using it, he turned the golden shaft upon the ground. The crowd murmured. Then suddenly the arrow twitched and turned itself Poleward again. The councilman dropped his stick, starting back with a cry. The others gasped. Caribou watched them.

"And these teeth," she said, touching the necklace about her neck. It rattled. "I wear them upon my breast by night and noon, and never take them off.

They speak to me, telling me always and ever the way. Just as my dreams speak to me. They will tell me surely the safe way to go."

She heard more murmurs, but they had lost their ugliness. The people still eyed her, but no longer in anger and wariness. The councilman was looking at her almost in awe. Here and there she saw a head nodding. Some of the children slept.

"We have already reached the Burning Plain's edge," she said to them, "which formerly it was said no one could ever cross. I have brought you safe so far. Will you not come with me the rest of the way?"

Again the murmurs, more of them this time, quieter now, no longer restless with fear. The stillness around her began to seem less ominous, the darkness now less wholly dark. Her body's warmth returned to Caribou. She knew they waited for some last word from her, to end it. Finally, she said:

"Who will sledge with me tomorrow along the reindeer's track?"

Slowly Djenret before her stirred. He glanced at her, then quickly about him as if gauging the others' thoughts. When he spoke, it was for all of them.

"We will sledge with you at daybreak, *i'dris.*"

The rest of the ring nodded silently, and those of the other rings as well.

"All of us will come." It was a young man's voice.

Turning, Caribou saw who had spoken: one of the youths on the sledge she and Reindeer had saved, the one who had been falling-down drunk on wine in Tjaalsénji, though today he had seemed sober enough.

He was not with his companions now. He could not have been much older than seventeen.

He sat just on the edge of her own circle, partly behind another traveler, his face mostly in shadow. She had not noticed him before. There was a red mark on his cheek where the gray water had burned him.

He did not seem to want to meet her eyes, but he had spoken with sincerity. For no reason, Caribou felt the hint of a smile edging the corner of her lips. Without thinking, she said something to cover it, but the youth had caught her smile. She saw him smiling a little in return.

"Eat, then," Caribou said, half over one shoulder at the others, but still looking at the youth. "Rest yourselves and sleep. Put out some of your fires once you have had done cooking. We must conserve our stores."

Caribou went back to her sledge and sat down. The people turned away, back to their own fires and food. Caribou cleaned out her cooled baking-bowl with moss. When she looked up, she saw the Tjaalsénji youth still watching her.

"Come here," she said. "I have a salve that will help your cheek."

He rose and came to her, knelt down again. Caribou did not search for the salve at once.

"Why did you come," she asked him, "you and your companions? I thought you followed Brakla in Tjaalsénji."

The youth blushed and looked down, away. His

hair and eyes were dark, his complexion olive. She had glimpsed shame on his face.

"You recognized us," he muttered.

Caribou put her cooking pot away. "Yes."

She waited then, let him realize she still wanted to know why he had come. The youth chafed his arms. He wore no *lanlan,* and was not very warmly dressed. Now that the flush had faded, his face seemed pale beneath its olive cast.

"We found the sledge," he murmured, "my friends and I. We didn't build it. The caribou, too. We found them. I think their owner must have gone to follow Nilsa or Vasli." He shook his head.

"Why did you come?" Caribou said again.

He looked back at her, his gaze full of pain suddenly.

"Val said we should go to the Open Hills, to see what the wisewoman would do, and the people there — for sport." He looked away again. "So we did, and watched your meeting, and ran with you a little way. Then the geyser split, and the woods were on fire. The caribou stampeded. The people on foot rushed for our sledge. So we fled with you into the canyon and came away."

The young man's voice had fallen to a whisper. Caribou rose and rummaged in the sledge to find the pot of salve she carried. "Why are you not with your friends now?"

The Tjaalsénji youth was standing now as well. He shook his head, put his hands beneath his armpits and shivered, shrugged. "When we halted tonight, they told me to go and not to come back." His voice tightened. "I had told them they could have killed us today — or you — racing on the snow. They are angry with me."

"You have foolish companions," Caribou said.

The young man breathed on his fingers, still looking away. She saw that he glanced back toward the oil fires, toward the people still eating from their pits.

"*I'dris,* I'm hungry," he said suddenly, so softly Caribou barely heard him.

She stared at him. "Did the three of you bring no food or supplies?"

He shook his head. "We weren't intending to come with you. We only meant to laugh at you on the Open Hills, and then go home."

His face crumpled for a moment, as though he might weep. But then he straightened and breathed deep, a little raggedly, still not looking at her. He was just a boy, really, Caribou found herself thinking. Only a boy.

"Here," she said, and handed him another of her cookpots from the sledge. "Put that on the fire." He would not take it from her at first, till she told him, "Don't worry. I brought enough."

He took it then, his face relaxing first into a look of relief, then gratitude.

"Did you bring anything to sleep on?" she asked him.

Blushing again, he shook his head.

"Well," she said. "I brought more skins than I need. Use these." She gave him some.

He simply stood there, holding the things she had given him. He looked up at last and gazed at her, and she at him. He had a beautiful, open face. She could not think who he reminded her of. He was tall for a youth, and would make a tall man in time.

"What is your name?" she asked him.

He answered, "Tor."

Caribou put her thumb in the pot of salve and touched it to the burn welt on his cheek. The hairs of his light, boy's beard were hardly sprung.

"Sledge with me tomorrow, Tor," she told him. "Don't go back to your friends."

The Tjaalsénji youth looked at her a moment more. He was of a slender build, his fingers long-made and strong-looking. It seemed to her that he wanted to say something more then, but after a moment, tongue-tied, he turned away and went back to the fire. He huddled over it, putting the cookpot on.

Caribou laid out her bedding on the ground. One by one she saw the oil-pots damped and taken up, until only a few in each circle remained. She let hers burn, for her lamp was filled with oil from the golden stag her brother had slain so long ago. In all this time it had never spoiled or been used up.

It seemed to burn without being consumed, a clear white flame, very hot. The salve she had put on Tor's cheek had been of the same stuff. The Tjaalsénji youth had finished his meal now, gone off somewhere to sleep. She searched but could not find him in the dark.

Caribou undressed in the flickering darkness, pulled off her boots and outer clothes, lay down upon her sleeping skins, and pillowed her head on her arm. By the dim light of the remaining oil-pots, she saw the others undressing and rolling into their sleeping skins, backs to the fire.

Caribou herself lay facing the fire. She did not sleep, but lay waking, longing for Reindeer and waiting for him to return. But now and again her thoughts wandered to Tor and his dark eyes that were not at all like Reindeer's eyes. Not expressionless at all.

14

Land's End

CARIBOU awakened the next morning before day-break to dress, roll up her bed, and pack the skins away. By the stray light of the few remaining oil-pots, she saw others doing the same. She had dreamed of Reindeer in his man-shape again, his yellow hair blazing.

In her dream, he was walking, leading a long file of caribou down a smooth, steep slope before striking out across a narrow bridge of land that spanned the black, watery sky. Lost in thought, Caribou stowed her bedroll in the *gristal,* feeling a sharp ache in her breast for Reindeer in his man-shape. She had no idea what the vision meant.

The people had gotten out their oil-pots again, arranging them in a circle and setting their long-legged bowls above them to cook the morning meal. She saw Tor huddled in the skins she had given him, beside a family from another sledge. He seemed to have begged his food from them this time, for he did not come to her. Caribou left him to himself.

She cooked her own meal and ate it in silence. Draft-caribou browsed on the reindeer moss. People sat on their heels about the flickering oil-pots, warming their hands and waiting for dawn. When daybreak came at last, all ash-gray light and cloud spread out in a long bar above the east horizon, Reindeer returned to the camp — as fresh and limber as if he had rested a week.

He vaulted the ring of *gristaal* effortlessly, and came on toward Caribou, shaking his golden pelt. The people fell back from him, murmuring. The caribou lifted their heads and looked. Caribou put her arms about her Reindeer's neck and leaned against him, laughing.

"So you are returned then, from your scouting," she said. "I never doubted, but some others among us did."

She felt his nose touching her shoulder and the hot cloud of his breath. Then he pulled free of her and went to stand before the sledge. Caribou scrubbed out her eating-bowl and put it up, blew out the oil-pot and stored that, too, then went to her golden stag to begin buckling the traces on.

"What did you see in your scouting?" she asked him.

He looked at her, but his great eyes told her nothing.

She lowered her voice and leaned nearer. "Can you give me no inkling?"

Frustration bit at her. How she wanted him in his man-shape again! Before her, the golden stag snorted, his breath twin jets of steam, and shook his head. Caribou sighed shortly and fastened the halter about his head, set the bit between his teeth, and brought the reins back to the sledge. He could speak no human words to her as he was.

When she reached the rear of the *gristal,* she found Tor standing there. He smiled at her shyly. He had scraped out the bowl she had given him the night before. Caribou smiled back as she took it. She pointed to a spot in the sledge-bed just before the driver's step.

"Sit there," she told him, "and muffle those skins about you. We will soon be past the Burning Plain, and your own light clothes will not be enough to keep you warm."

The youth obeyed, using the thongs she handed him to lash himself to the sledge beneath the skins. Reindeer had turned and now stood looking at them with his great golden eyes. He cavaled, but Caribou only clacked the reins at him, clicking her tongue and calling, "Oh, why do you caval? He is only a boy that has no *gristal* to ride on. Would you begrudge him that?"

Tor stared at Reindeer, his dark eyes uncertain, his face a little pale, till Caribou touched her passenger's shoulder. He flushed as she murmured for him to be easy. After that he gazed only at Caribou. All around them, the others were breaking camp.

Reindeer watched both of them a moment more, then turned and stood still, save for a furious shaking of his hide in the traces — till the bells sang like a shower of gold — and after that, a slow, measured picking at the turf with one great, splay hoof.

They set off southward toward the Pole, in the direction the reindeer had run, toward the dim horizon over which that silver hoard had disappeared, toward the point where the red glow, now invisible, had hung in the darkness the night before.

As on the previous day, the sledges fanned out behind Caribou's lead, Reindeer drawing their own *gristal* far to the fore. They went swiftly and steadily, but with none of the wild rush of their first day's running. All was gray silence, which the chanting of the bells in Reindeer's harness only seemed to magnify.

As the hidden sun came up, the day growing gradually light enough to distinguish gray land from gray-colored sky, Caribou could see that indeed the land had changed. The terrain was hillier, frost-dry, and barren but for the reindeer moss and some lichen. The land spread in wrinkled tundra, and it was cold. No warmth seeped up in steam from beneath these hills. They had passed beyond the Burning Plain.

People latched their *lanlani* about their throats and tightened the wrists of their sleeves, muffled their faces with wool-woven scarfs. Gradually, they approached the low line of black hills they had seen by the last of yesterday's light.

They were loose drifts, their surface tiny bits of brittle cinders, black as burnt sugar, though here and there dusted with white snow like crumbled tallow. Their sledges moved sluggishly over the soft, sifting stuff, the caribou struggling to keep their footing.

From time to time, passengers had to spring down to shoulder their landboats over the rough places. Only Reindeer seemed able to pick his way over the black dunes with ease. They slogged for hours, the land rising gradually and the air growing drier and thin as a knife. The caribou labored getting up the slopes, their breath thick, white clouds.

At length, near noon, Caribou perceived an edge to the Cinderlands ahead, a point beyond which she saw only sky marking the high point of the dunes, beyond which the land must slope downward again. She did not guess how steeply till Reindeer drew even with the crest of the hill.

Caribou started, and heard her passenger draw breath. She reined in, reflexively, though Reindeer had already stopped. Lifting her golden arrow, she motioned for the *gristaal* behind to come on, slowly. They halted in a long line on either side.

The land before them fell sharply away, as steeply as the crisp, sliding cinders would allow. What lay beyond was a great, level reach of land — the same black grit — while far in the distance on either side lay the flat, silvery sea. Cold, foaming, and salt, it battered itself in white breakers against the black beachhead.

A long river of calmer water reached from the cliffs directly below toward the horizon straight ahead. No ultimate sea was visible there. The river-course steamed, hissing like boiling broth. Geysers of white cloud spouted and subsided; their spray hung in the air. The end of the narrow neck of land was obscured by fog.

Caribou heard a woman behind her exclaim, "Is that what we must cross, that skinny arm of land between two seas, with a hot ditch down the middle of it?"

"No other way south unless you'd swim," a man's voice called.

Caribou drew breath to speak.

"But how shall we even get down to it?" she heard a youth's voice saying quietly, very near. She realized it was Tor. He sat shaking his head. "The reindeer made their way down, and the caribou — see their tracks? — but they were not encumbered by sleds."

He glanced at her, his dark eyes frowning. Caribou laid her hand on his shoulder for the second time that day and smiled. Her dream of the night before was beginning to come clear. She turned, her golden arrow raised, to address the others.

"Follow me," she bade them, "in a single file, slowly. We will descend in long switchbacks, doubling back on our course, but lower down the slope each time. Be not dismayed. My golden stag will lead you. Everything proceeds as I have dreamed."

At her signal, Reindeer started down the steep, slippery slope. He picked his way carefully, mindful of the heavier sledges behind. Drivers tied up their reins and walked beside their teams, but Caribou stayed on the driver's stand, letting Reindeer choose his own pace and way.

When at last they reached the bottom of the black cinder slope, Caribou called a halt to allow the others to catch up. Here the long black arm of land stretched out into the sea, and the long reach of water swirled in a wide pool under the cliffs. Caribou gazed at the shallow cave in the rock — hardly more than an overhang — and felt a sudden puzzlement, for she could see no hollow deep enough for any underground water-source.

Before her, Tor knelt upon the black shingle bank. He held his hand above the steaming water a moment, then swiftly dipped one finger in. When he touched its tip to his tongue, Caribou saw his eyes widen. He raised his head to glance at her, then dipped his hand again and rose. Coming to her, he let her taste.

"This water is neither sweet nor mineral," she exclaimed, "but salt."

Caribou gazed out to sea. Suddenly she understood: the water in the trough did not run outward, oceanward, from the land, but inland from the horizon toward the hills with an ebb and flow of crestless waves that had carved out the underside of the cliff. She turned to Tor again.

"This channel is no river-course, but a long firth of the sea."

Before her, in the traces, Reindeer snorted and stamped. His silent breath came in rapid little bursts, so that if she had not known he had no human heart, she would have sworn he was laughing at them — that they had taken so long in puzzling it out, and seemed so taken with wonder at the discovery.

Caribou pursed her lips with a twinge of vexation, but she let it go. She would not quarrel with her *trangl* now. When all the sledges had assembled at the foot of the slope, she motioned Tor aboard and whistled

Reindeer into a trot. He went docilely enough, following the reindeer tracks southward along the left bank of the boiling firth.

They traveled at a rapid pace until the early afternoon, the broad stretch of land on which they fared growing gradually narrower, until a heavy bank of fog enveloped them. Caribou did not slow; rather, she called out over one shoulder, "My bells! Follow the chant of my Reindeer's bells."

Behind her she heard cries of assent, and thereafter she heard the drivers of the other sledges talking and calling to one another. Caribou smiled, for their voices told her that her people had once more taken heart.

By midafternoon the fog had passed. The sky overhead arched high and clear, with scarves of cold, white cloud scudding the blue. The wind was crisp and salt and chill, the sun poised halfway down the sky, white as flame. The land ran on and on.

Then all at once ahead of them lay the end of the land. The firth opened and shallowed, joining the sea. The bank on the right seemed to fall away steeply; their own leftward bank, much more gradually. She saw the uncountable reindeer tracks on the black shingle shore disappearing into the waves.

Reindeer stopped at the water's edge. Caribou heard the others pulling up behind. The cold sun shone brilliant in her eyes as she studied the water. The currents ran swift and treacherous over the shoal. Her people were not like the River-Valley Folk; they knew nothing of boats.

No shore lay in sight beyond the waves, only a

little promontory of standing stones jutting from the
water a few score paces down the beach. Herds of
sea-beasts that barked like dogs glided in flocks through
the shallows. Small, ice-encrusted islands rose from
the sea to east and west — and then Caribou saw they
were not rock at all.

They were moving: floating chunks of ice that
gleamed beneath the sun like palaces of polished bone.
She stared at them, at all of it, astonished — until all
at once she realized that the people behind her were
arguing, had been arguing for some time now while
she had gazed. Caribou turned to face them.

"And what do we do now?" one driver was demanding of another, older woman, a council member.
Caribou remembered her: Brikka, the one with beads
in her hair.

"You see?" another driver interjected, gesturing with
his willow whip. "I was right. They are all *traangol*,
the reindeer, and can run upon the waves."

"Or swim the running sea, like those seadogs there,"
an old man cried.

Caribou glanced back at the bright, breaking waves.
Some of the seadogs had stopped their frolic, hung
upright in the water, their sleek, dark heads turned
toward the shore, their black eyes curious.

Caribou sighed and turned toward her people again.
More drivers and passengers had come down from
their sledges to approach the councilwoman. Above
the general clamor, Caribou finally heard Brikka exclaim, "Enough, enough! Let us hear what our wisewoman says."

"Yes," Djenret of Vlad called. "Our *i'dris* will know."

But Caribou did not know. Her heart felt tight with fear. She had no idea why the land had ended. Her dreams had shown her nothing of this, only Reindeer crossing a landbridge that stretched the length of the sky to the other side of the world.

She glanced at her *trangl,* but he only gazed back and chivied at the water's edge. Though his gold eyes were as expressionless as ever, telling her nothing, she sensed he was as baffled as she. All eyes had turned to Caribou. On her own sledge, Tor had turned to her as well.

"*I'dris,*" the young man said, "what must we do?"

Other voices echoed his. Caribou tasted the salt breeze on her lips, eyeing the little promontory of rock standing out from shore.

"I must think on it," she answered. "We must wait."

15

Trolls' Hedge

CARIBOU got down from her sledge and bade Tor and the others do the same. She told them to stretch their legs, or rest, or eat if they felt hungry, or tend to their caribou. Then she unbuckled Reindeer from his bells and walked with him a little way down the beach that she might speak with him alone.

"You know nothing of this, do you?" she asked him, stroking his neck and ears as he stood before her.

Reindeer snorted and tossed his head, gazing out to sea where the reindeer tracks led. Caribou, too, gazed.

"Can you not speak?" she whispered, unable to keep the urgency from her voice. She nodded toward the cluster of rocks that stood off from shore a little way. "We could go out to that promontory there. You could put on your man-shape and tell me what you know."

Her fingers in his thick golden fur tightened, but Reindeer pulled away from her and pawed at the beach, glancing back toward the others and their *gristaal*. Tor had just climbed down from their own sledge and was stretching. Caribou sighed.

"I must dream on it, then. But not here. I will go out to the rocks." She held out her hand to Reindeer, although in his deer-shape he could not take it. "Come with me."

The golden *trangl* only shook himself and did not look at her. He stood watching the others. Far away, Tor was kneeling to pick up a stone from the beach. Rising, he threw it into the sea. Caribou bit her lip in frustration and turned back to Reindeer. She sighed again.

"Well," she said at last. "You know best whether you can help me in this or not. I see it is my turn, now, to scout the way."

Reluctantly, Caribou walked away from her *trangl*. She followed a sandbar across the chill, shallow salt water toward the tiny island of rock. Approaching, she saw with a little start that it was a trolls' hedge, a circle of standing stones shaped like a fort or crown.

The rocks looked oddly familiar somehow. The sandbar's path led to a low place between two taller rocks, and she realized that she must either enter the hedge or remain standing in the shallow sea. There was no beach at all about the stones. So, reciting under her breath a charm against offending the daimons, Caribou climbed between the stones.

The interior was exactly as she recalled that other trolls' hedge, the one that had sheltered her and Reindeer the night his father had borne him away. Little steam-vents in the bare, flat ground misted up warm wisps of cloud. Caribou sat down. After the bracing sea-breeze and the motion of the sledge all morning long, the warmth and stillness of this sheltered air made her suddenly sleepy. She let her eyelids slip shut.

After a little time, she heard all around her a rustling and a sighing. Opening her eyes, she found that the stones of the hedge seemed to be shifting, jostling where they stood. A moment later, when her vision had cleared, she saw that she was surrounded not by stones at all anymore, but by a dozen great crouching trolls.

Or rather, she realized in panic, the stones had always been trolls, only they had been sitting so still in their drab gray garb, their heads nodded and their eyelids closed, as if napping, that she had not been able to tell till now what they were.

They had great, coarse hands and long noses, and little eyes. But they smiled at her with their huge stonelike teeth, and seemed to be at pains not to frighten her. Caribou sat very still.

"Do you remember us?" one of them said. She held a squat clay pipe in her teeth like a shaman, and smoked. "We are hedgewives."

Caribou realized with a start that they were all women.

"We remember you," one sitting beside the first one said. Her voice sounded very like the sighing of a steam-vent, or sea-surf, or wind. "You are the little one who stayed with us before, a long time ago, and suckled the *trangl*'s child."

"I meant no trespass," said Caribou hastily, "then or now." She had to swallow, her throat was so dry.

The hedgewives nodded. One of them answered, "We did not begrudge you your stay." She spoke slowly, as though not familiar with mortal speech. "Though your presence that night did keep us from gambling —"

"We are very fond of gambling," the hedgewife with the clay pipe said.

"In any case, we had already dined for the day," her sister continued, "and saw no need to trouble you."

"Besides, you had the little *trangl* with you," another said, "whose father had died. The *traangol* are daimons, as we are, and so for his sake we did not disturb you."

She put her teeth together with the crushing sound of rock rubbing rock, and smiled. Caribou shivered, and wondered if the hedgewives had dined yet *this* day, and whether or not they would be so kindly disposed toward her now that her *trangl* was no longer with her.

"But what has brought you back to us?" one of the trolls behind her asked, so that Caribou started and turned around — she had forgotten they surrounded her.

Before she could answer, the troll continued, "We were on our way across the landbridge, away from the troubled country where we used to dwell — but we stopped to take our rest and gamble a little, and the reindeer passed us by. So now it will be spring before we can get across."

Caribou felt her heartbeat beginning to quicken,

but it was from hope now, not fear. "Daimons," she said, "my people, too, are on their way across, away from the troubled earth. But what has happened to the land? How did the reindeer get across?"

"Ah." The hedgewives nodded. "The firelords have lowered the bridge so that the sea covers it, for the reindeer have already passed, and the *waijen* must not be allowed to get back across."

"Every year a few *waijen* manage it," one of the trollwomen put in, "to wander again in their old country and haunt the people they do not love. But not many. The firelords guard their landbridge well."

"Except three winters back," another hedgewife cried, laughing and jabbing her sister with the stem of her pipe. "When the sea-maidens sang the bridge-man to sleep before he had lowered the bridge again — and as many of the *waijen* as pleased flocked back across into the land of the living again. Such a ghostly winter we had!"

Caribou remembered the first winter after Reindeer had left her, and all the *waijen* that had roamed about her *ntula,* and those of her father and Branja that had spoken to her. She turned back from her thoughts to the trollwomen sitting around her.

"Then I must go to the firelords and ask them to raise the bridge again," Caribou said, "so that I and my people may cross. Can you tell me where I may find them?"

At that the hedgewives shifted and grumbled among themselves, and she heard some of them grinding their teeth.

"We could," one of them said. "We know where they dwell. But perhaps —" She leaned closer to Caribou. "But perhaps you could give us something in return?"

Though the hedgewives still smiled, they had all leaned closer now, looming over Caribou.

"We have not dined for the day," one of them said.

Caribou started quickly to her feet — she knew well enough from the stories her father had told her, what food such daimons were fondest of. But seeing her alarm, the trollwomen all leaned back a little, and Caribou's panic eased. She made herself breathe deep.

"We have no *pisjlak* to spare," she said firmly.

"Well, a few of your caribou, then?" one of the hedgewives suggested.

"We have no spare caribou," Caribou answered. "They all ran on the heels of the reindeer."

The hedgewives grumbled.

"Perhaps a few of your people . . . ?" the one holding the pipe began, but Caribou quickly cut her off.

"No, they would not consent. I promised to bring them all safe away, all of them."

The thought of these trollwomen feasting on the marrow of her people's bones chilled her. The hedgewives muttered and consulted among themselves. Caribou stood taut, straining, but could not distinguish what they said. Their great brows frowned above their little eyes. Unease gripped her. Then, all at once, one of the trollwomen said to another, "Perhaps the mortal woman will gamble for it."

"Ah," the others all said, beginning to smile again. "Perhaps she will gamble for it." They turned back to Caribou. "Take the dice out of your sash, little one, and we will all have a throw. If you win, we will tell you the way to the firelords and ask nothing in return."

Caribou's hand went to her sash, and there, to her surprise, she felt the hard lumps of the three dice she had carved from the golden stag's horns. She drew them out, unable to fathom it, for she did not remember having put them in her sash that morning when she dressed. She turned the little forms over in her hand.

"And if I lose?" she asked them softly.

"Then you must give us your bones," the hedge-wives said.

Caribou shuddered, her stomach knotting. The sour taste of bile rose in her throat. The hedgewives nodded cheerfully, expectantly. Caribou swallowed and fought her revulsion down. *I must do this,* she told herself. *There is no other way.* Her fingers closed around the dice. *If I do not find my way to the firelords and persuade them to raise the bridge, we are all dead in any case.*

So Caribou played the trollwomen at dice. Shaking the cube, the flattened cylinder, and the many-sided piece in her hands, she called out what marks she hoped for — foxpaws, or pigeons' wings, or snakes' tongues, or one of each — and then the hedgewives each in turn did the same.

Every time Caribou shook the dice, she listened to

the rattle of the golden stag's teeth against her breast, for they whispered to her how the throw would fall. By the time the dice had passed once around the circle, Caribou had won every throw and the hedgewives not a one. They grumbled even louder then, and one of them cried, "Those dice are weighted."

"They are not," Caribou replied, "else they would have fallen the same on every throw, and the same for you as they did for me. In any case, you chose the dice, not I."

The first of the hedgewives, the one who held the pipe, nodded with a sigh. "Aye. Sisters, she has spoke the truth. Fair is fair, and we agreed. Here, little one. Here is the way to the firelords. We have been sitting at the gate all along."

She leaned down and touched the earth with her pipe, and suddenly, soundlessly — without so much as a rumble or a tremor — the ground opened before Caribou like the mouth of a sack. A long tunnel led down into the dimness, its under-surface cut into steps.

"Just follow the stair," the trollwoman said. "It will take you straight to the firelords' hall."

"The way forks once," another hedgewife added, "but take the right-hand fork, and you will not go wrong."

Then the trollwomen all smiled and nodded at her, seeming suddenly much happier than they had been, so that Caribou was suspicious. But she could do no other than follow their advice. She turned and stepped into the darkness of the tunnel, and started down the stair.

Caribou descended — for a long time, it seemed. She quickly lost count of the steps. The way was lit, dimly, by a reddish-yellow glow, though she could not tell the source. The deeper she went, the warmer the air became, so that she had to unfasten her *lanlan,* and then remove it entirely, take off her cap and mitts, and finally her leggings. She loosened the laces at the throat of her smock and rolled up the sleeves.

At first she tried to carry all her garments with her, but since there were so many they were very cumbersome. At length she left them on the steps, along with her smock and boots. By the time she came to the fork in the stair, she wore only the inner slippers of her boots and her shift.

She stood a long moment at the fork, listening, for it seemed that far below them, to the left, she could hear faint noises of laughter and merriment. But she took the right-hand branch in the end, as the hedge-wives had instructed, though its passage seemed darker than the left-hand one, and very silent, too.

Again Caribou descended for a very long time, but at last, reaching the bottom of the steps, she found herself within a few paces of a great square arch made of carved whalebone, such as the chieftain of the whole Tribe might have set before his house.

Beyond the archway stood a great winch and tackle of wood, such as workers might raise a roof beam with, the cable for which, thick as a child's body, rose

away into the darkness above. Near it rose a vast
building like a chieftain's house or a meeting hall, save
that it was made of chiseled stone and not of wood.
Though she craned her neck, Caribou could not see
any roof topping the walls.

So intent was she on these things as she approached
that she did not notice the figure dozing against the
arch until she was almost upon him. He awoke with
a start and sat up sputtering. Caribou swallowed her
own surprise.

"Good greetings," she told him courteously.

He only blinked and stared at her. "Hie," he huffed
at last, "I didn't think to be disturbed till spring, when
the reindeer come again. What right have you —" He
lumbered to his feet suddenly, peering at her. "You're
not a sea-maid, are you?"

Caribou shook her head. "No, I am a mortal woman
who has come to beg a boon of the Fireking. Are you
one of his lords?"

She asked this uncertainly, for there was nothing
fiery about the one who stood before her. He was of
no great height — barely as tall as Caribou — but he
had legs thick as tree boles and was twice as broad
across the ribs and shoulders as any mortal man, with
great blunt hands, no hair on his pate at all, and long,
slanting eyes. He appeared immensely strong, strong
enough to turn the enormous winch beyond the gate.

"A firelord?" the other boomed, and his laughter
sounded like a great tree creaking. "I'm only the
bridgeman, mortal, their gatekeeper."

"The bridgeman?" Caribou exclaimed. The hedge-wives had not told her that her path would lead to the bridgeman himself, only that it would take her to the Fireking. Her heart leapt with hope. Perhaps she need go no farther. "I and my people are fleeing the country where the firelords have wakened the earth," she told him. "We wish to pass across to the land beyond, where the reindeer winter. Will you raise the bridge?"

The bridgeman, peering at her again with his long, narrow eyes, gave a disgruntled sigh. "You come from the land north of here? Yes, I see now you are not a sea-maid. Slippery thieves! They made a fool of me once."

He folded his powerful arms.

"My masters would never pardon me a second time if I kept the bridge up out of season. I will not raise it. The bridge cannot go up again till spring. You will have to wait." He closed his eyes and settled himself back down to doze.

"But we cannot wait," cried Caribou. "The cold will kill us. We will starve."

The bridgeman shrugged. "It is none of my affair. I can do nothing for you without my masters' word."

"Where are your masters, then, that I may speak with them?" demanded Caribou. "How may I find them?"

"They are in the hall," the bridgeman replied, nodding over one shoulder. But when Caribou came forward to pass through the arch, he held up one large square hand. "Not so swiftly, mortalwoman. There is the matter of my toll. None enter the hall of the Fireking without paying."

Caribou stopped short. She had never heard of such a thing, and she had nothing to pay with now but her slippers and shift. "What must I pay?"

"Oh, anything you please," the gatekeeper replied, "so long as it is to my liking."

Caribou knelt down on the stone path, frowning hard, trying to think what lay in her power to offer the bridgeman.

"I can tell you a tale," she began, "for my father taught me many before he died . . ."

The gateman only laughed. "Oh, tales. I have heard more tales than time can count, as many as there ever were in the world, for that is what the *waijen* pay me with when they cross the bridge." He settled himself a little more comfortably. "There was such a crowd of them clamoring at my gate not long ago!"

For a moment Caribou thought of the rest of her Tribe, all the people that had been left behind in the land where she had dwelled. Had they all perished and become *waijen*? Her stomach clenched.

The same thing will happen to the people in my care, those who wait on the beach above, she thought, *if I do not find a toll to pay this bridgeman. Then how many more* waijen *will be clamoring at his gate?*

The gatekeeper sighed. "I can tell you the ending of any tale that has ever been told," he grunted, "before you have said a dozen words."

Caribou thought again, determined. "Have you a

dream to be interpreted?" she asked. "I have done that, too, in the country from which I come."

The firelords' bridgeman only shook his head. "I am a daimon, mortal. I do not dream."

She grimaced. Frustration made her ribs feel tight. "Then have you lost anything? I can tell you where to look for it."

But again, no. "Oh, I own next to nothing," he said, "and it is all safe in my keeping still."

Caribou racked her brains. "Do you need advice?" she asked. "I can advise you whom best to marry, or which of your children to leave your goods to . . ."

The bridgeman shrugged. "Those are mortal concerns, all of them, and have no meaning for me. You will have to do better."

Caribou bit her lip, nearly frantic. She had no idea how long she had been away from her people, gambling with the hedgewives above, then descending the steps and arguing with the bridgeman here below. There were stories she had heard of mortals who had come into the company of daimons. Sometimes such mortals were gone for years, though it had seemed only moments to them, or for only moments, though it had seemed years and years.

A sudden image came to her of her people many seasons dead, and their bones rotting on the sand — but then she realized it must be only fear that made her think of that, and not true vision, for the reindeer had not yet returned to cross the bridge again. Relief overwhelmed her. She felt weak. No, it could not be spring yet, for the reindeer had not returned. The teeth on her breast rattled and clicked, and all at once Caribou felt her desperation subside.

"You say you know every tale that is," she said to the bridgeman, "but I know one you have not heard — and you are in the tale."

The bridgeman sat up abruptly and ceased his yawning. "I have never heard a tale wherein I played a part," he told her, then grinned with teeth that looked like white ash wood. "Tell on."

So Caribou told him the tale of the *trangl*'s child that she had raised, and how he had gone away, then returned to lead her people away from the restless earth; how they had crossed the Burning Plain and come to Land's End, how she had gambled with the hedgewives, then descended toward the Fireking's hall, and had spoken with the gateman there, and begun to tell him a tale . . .

"But why have you stopped?" the square-shouldered daimon cried out. He had been listening, rapt, with all appearance of delight, until Caribou reached that point and ceased to speak. "What happens next? I do not know the ending of this tale."

Caribou sighed. "Nor do I. Nor will it have an end, unless you let me pass your gate into the Fireking's hall. This tale is not finished yet."

The gatekeeper frowned, gnashing his wooden teeth, but at last he answered. "So. Aye. I suppose I must let you through. *Hmpf.* But you must promise to give me the ending when you come out again."

Caribou rose, almost laughing with relief. "When

next I pass through your gate," she promised, "I will tell you the rest."

He allowed her to walk by him then, under the whalebone arch, beside the great winch governing the landbridge, which no mortal hand could ever have turned, and on through the doorway of the great gray stone building, into the hall of the Fireking.

16

The Fireking

THE HALL was vast, bright-lit, all one great room, with the roof beams so high in the shadows above that Caribou could not see them, the walls so far away on either hand that she could scarcely discern them, and the other end ahead of her so distant she could barely make it out. Caribou stood wonderstruck.

At last she set out across the great stone hall, her feet making no echo at all upon the floor, toward those who must be the firelords. They stood in council at the far end. One of their number sat in a chair upon a platform with steps, and Caribou guessed he must be the Fireking.

She passed without a word among the other daimons that stood about the hall conversing, or sat at table, or made music: tall, willowy *iffs*, and squat, prickly *onts*, yellow pool-sprites steaming and smelling of sulfur, fire-daimons, and other creatures so strange she could not put a name to them. Uncertain how they might take her curiosity, Caribou tried not to stare. But none of them paid her any attention.

She felt uneasy in their midst, ragged, almost a beggar, and she wished keenly that Reindeer had consented to come with her. He was a daimon, and would know how to carry himself among such as these. But Reindeer was not here. She would have to deal with the firelords on her own — *as I have dealt with the hedgewives and the bridgekeeper,* she told herself. Even so, as she crossed the seemingly endless hall, she was trembling.

She drew near the firelords at last. They stood twice her height and more, their fine garb all black and umber, a fiery reddish glow about their skin and hair, like dying coals. Caribou knelt, but they were deeply absorbed in some debate, arguing before their chief, and took no note of her.

"O firelords," Caribou cried, loudly. The great hall surrounded her words and swallowed them. "O Fireking, I have come to ask a mercy of you."

The firelords who had been debating with their king upon his chair turned and looked at her, surprised.

"And what has the gateman let in this time?" one of them said.

"I daresay he was asleep, and this slipped past," the other mused.

Caribou shook her head and tried to keep her voice steady. "I gave him a toll that was to his liking, and so he let me through."

Some of the firelords murmured then, and the two who had been debating crossed their arms in displeasure, but the man on the great, raised chair waved them all to silence.

"We will continue what we were arguing once we have seen to this." He leaned toward Caribou. "What are you, little one?"

His skin was black and hard-looking as cooled earthrock, glowing red along the creases and seams. His eyes were yellow, like an oil lamp's flame, and his hair and his beard were like burning fire. Caribou's mouth was dry.

"Lord, I am a mortal woman," she whispered.

"Mortal?" the Fireking asked. "What is that? I have not heard of that race."

Caribou sat a moment, frowning, and a little of her fear subsided into puzzlement. Though she had never heard of the firelords before Reindeer had told her, it had never occurred to her that the firelords might not have heard of her Tribe.

"Our kind pass over the landbridge after death," she began, but the Fireking murmured, "Death," as though he did not know what it meant.

Caribou tried again. "They come this way and tell your gateman tales to let them cross the bridge."

"Oh, *waijen*," the Fireking said. "But they are gaunt and ghostly things. You do not look like a *wajn* to me."

Caribou shook her head. "Not *waijen,* lord. We are . . ." She struggled. "We are what the *waijen* are before they become the *waijen*."

"Strange."

"We come from the country north of here, beyond the Burning Plain."

"Ah." The Fireking smiled. "I know your country. Where the *traangol* summer and calve."

Relief made Caribou flush. She nodded. "Lord, the *traangol* say your people have wakened the earth there."

The other answered, "Yes. I have sent my work-men there to stir the earth, and turn it, for it is time for the land there to change its mantle. We have mined all the gold and precious silver from it that we can, and now must make it new again."

Caribou's uneasiness returned, for she understood no more of this than when she had heard the same from Reindeer, but she continued, "My lord, your turning of the earth has forced my people to flee our homeland."

"I know nothing of that."

"Lord, we wish to go where the *traangol* winter, beyond the Pole to another country where the earth rests peaceful still. We wish to cross the bridge."

She waited then, expectant, hanging on his silence. Surely no ruler could refuse so worthy a request. She thought of her people waiting on the beach. How long had she been gone? She must get back to them . . . All at once dismay filled her. The Fireking was shaking his head.

"That cannot be," he said. "The gateman has al-ready lowered the bridge. It may not be raised again until spring."

Desperation brought Caribou to her feet. "But we will die if you make us wait until spring," she cried. "The cold will kill us. My people will starve."

"Cold?" the Fireking said. "You find the world above us cold?"

"It is cold to *us,* my lord . . ."

"And starve?" the Fireking asked. "How may you starve in the midst of so much earth and snow?"

"We do not eat that, lord."

The Fireking did not seem to hear. "But what is 'die'?" he said, frowning. "I do not understand what you mean by that."

Caribou wrung her hands. The lives of her people depended on her being able to persuade the Fireking.

"Become *waijen,*" she exclaimed, barely able to contain her frustration now.

"Why do you not become *waijen?*" he asked her. "Then you would not mind the wait, or the cold and starving."

"But we do not *wish* to become *waijen,*" Caribou insisted, groping. "It . . . it is not the time."

"Hmm," the Fireking said, running his stone-black fingers through his beard of fire, "very strange. You are fragile creatures indeed if you do not like the cold and must eat other things besides earth and snow."

"We cannot help that, lord," said Caribou softly.

"Why did you not come when the reindeer passed?"

"We tried, lord, but the reindeer outran us."

"The reindeer?" the Fireking exclaimed. "They are hardly even as swift as the wind. If even the reindeer outpaced you, then your people are very slow."

"Lord," Caribou told him, feeling a helplessness bordering on despair, "we go as quickly as we can."

"Hmm," the Fireking said, musing, "well — what would you have me do?"

"Command the gatekeeper to raise the bridge and let us pass!" she cried.

But the Fireking only laughed. "Oh, I could command him, mortalwoman, but I doubt that he would follow my command."

"What, how do you mean?" exclaimed Caribou, gathering courage to go closer to him. Her people's need made her bold. "Are you not his master? Must he not obey when you command?"

The king of the firelords shrugged. "His master? More or less. As much as any of us is master of another. But I tell you, he will not raise the bridge till spring, no matter what I ask. He cannot."

Caribou stared at him.

"It is a mighty task even for one so square and strong as he," the Fireking said, "and the bridgeman can manage it only once every season, winter and spring, and then must rest the next half-year until he has grown strong enough again."

"But . . . the sea-maidens . . ." Caribou stammered.

The Fireking snorted. "Them. Oh, they sang him to sleep one year before he could lower the bridge after the reindeer had passed. He had not raised it especially for them."

Caribou's heart grew very still. Her ribs tightened, and she could get no air. "But why . . ." she began, "why did he not tell me this when I spoke with him?"

The Fireking smiled. "I imagine he wanted your toll."

Daimons, said Caribou to herself, furious, thinking of the bridgeman, of the hedgewives, of the golden stag that had been Reindeer's father — charming Branja and stealing her child. *And Reindeer,* she thought suddenly, with a pulse of fear, *is he, too, treacherous — a deceiver, as Branja's* wajn *said?* The old tales of her father always spoke of the daimons as perilous. Caribou's legs felt weak.

"But," she said all at once, observing once more the Fireking's size and strength, "are *you* not strong enough, my lord — might *you* not turn the winch? Your kind have the power to shake mountains and rend the earth. Surely you have might enough —"

Sudden hope had brought the vigor back into her voice. The Fireking rose, coming down from his chair, and drew near Caribou. She felt the terrible heat of him, and flinched, afraid. Kneeling, he showed her his hands. The backs of them were crusted and cool, but the palms blazed red as liquid stone.

"Mortalwoman," he said, "were I to touch the Winch of Wood, it would be destroyed, and then the bridge might never be raised or lowered again. None but the gateman may turn that wheel, for it is of a stuff very like himself and responds to him alone. No other daimon has this power."

He sighed then, and seemed to shrug — the burning air about him shimmered so that it was hard for Caribou to be certain. Rising, he turned and went back to his chair. Hope died in Caribou. She felt sick and faint from the heat.

"I wish that I might help you, mortalwoman," the Fireking remarked, "but there is nothing I can do."

Slowly, Caribou turned away from the Fireking. She could scarcely see, blinded by heat and tears. She heard the firelords behind her resuming their debate as she stumbled away toward the far entrance of the hall.

What more could she do? The landbridge could not be raised until spring. Her people would perish. *Better,* she raged bitterly, *better to have left them all to perish — to have perished with them at the start — than to have held out to them this hope of rescue, now destroyed.*

As she neared the wide entrance to the hall, she passed a little crowd of women she had not noticed before. They were not much taller than she, though very long and slender. Their hair was wet and yellow-green, and they were clothed all in some dripping, filmy stuff that was neither of skin nor of woven cloth.

It clung to them and hid their legs, so that Caribou, blinking and staring, was not able to tell whether they had legs at all, or fishes' tails. Their garb left pools of water where they stood. One of them caught Caribou's hand as she went by. Her touch was damp and very cold. Another touched her arm.

"Mortalwoman," one of them said, and another: "*I'dris.* Caribou."

Caribou stopped and looked at them. "You know my name."

"Yes," they answered. "We know of you. Even so far away in our home in the sea, there are tales of you, for all rivers flow there, and everything comes down to the sea in the end. We are the sea-maidens, and we have heard of you."

"You are the one who suckled the *trangl*'s child,"

another said, "and brought him back to you after he had gone away."

"And have kept him beside you for a whole season, not just for a night."

"How lucky you are," the sea-women sighed. "We envy you."

"What do you want?" said Caribou curtly. She did not trust any of the daimons anymore. *Except Reindeer,* she told herself fiercely: *Reindeer, whom I love.*

"We want to help you," all the women-of-the-sea replied. "Only that, and no deceit. We heard your petition to the Fireking."

Caribou turned away. "You know my people's plight is hopeless, then."

"No, no," the sea-women cried. "Not hopeless. We can help."

"Why?" demanded Caribou, taking her hand from the sea-maiden's cool, wet clasp. "Why should daimons wish to help me?"

"Because we know what it is to crave another so much that it is hard to bear, and yet have the one we crave remain indifferent."

Caribou frowned, uncertain what they meant.

"We crave the firelords," another sea-maiden said, "though they will not come to us. Each night we sing to them and woo them, but all in vain. They say we long only to quench and devour them."

"It is not so," her sister beside her said. "They burn so hot it is we, not they, who would be consumed in a flash if ever they allowed us to embrace them and kiss them."

"But they will not. And so we crave them still, and sigh."

"But you," one of the sea-women said, "you have succeeded where we have failed. We see how you have bound the young *trangl* to you . . ."

"But . . . I do not bind him," Caribou said, surprised. "I love him. He came back to me because he wanted to."

"Love?" the sea-maidens asked her. "What is love?"

And Caribou remembered how Reindeer had asked her the same question once, a long time ago. Could she answer any better now?

"It is . . ." she began, then sighed. How to tell them? They were not mortal. Would they understand her any more than Reindeer had? "It is a longing — but true love has no wish to bind. I know that I can never hold Reindeer against his will. I tried to once." She blushed with shame. "But never again. That was not love."

The sea-maidens listened, rapt, saying nothing. Caribou groped. She had no idea how to express to them what she felt for Reindeer. She tried again.

"When I am with him, though I may be sad, my sadness seems lighter. His presence brings me happiness. And I want never to cause him sorrow, only joy . . ."

There she stopped herself, realizing. *But see how I think of him still,* still *as though he were a mortal man. And what does he think,* she wondered. *How does he think of me? He is a daimon, as these sea-maidens are. Does he understand anything of what*

I feel for him? Does he return it? How can I ever know?

"Joy?" the women-of-the-sea replied. "Sorrow? We know nothing of these things."

Caribou looked down. The way they echoed Reindeer's words made her feel oddly, incongruously like laughing. It came out almost a sob. "Nor does he." She feared that was the truth.

"He does not feel this love, this sorrow, as you do?" the one who had taken her hand asked Caribou.

She shook her head, at a loss. What did she really know of Reindeer? "I think . . . I think that he can know only a feeling of loss, never sorrow — no sort of love, only desire." Did she really believe that? The sea-women watched her. She looked at them bitterly. "He is a daimon. Like you. He cannot."

She was weeping again. The sea-maidens stood silent, lost in their own thoughts. After a time, the tears stopped and Caribou sighed. She felt very tired.

"How can you help me?" she asked them at last. "The Fireking said the landbridge cannot be raised."

"Oh, it cannot," one of the maidens replied. "That is not what we propose. Even now the bridge does not lie so very deep beneath the waves."

The sea-maid who had touched Caribou's arm said, "We can sing the sea away from the bridge for a little while, leaving the way dry, or nearly so."

"Then you could cross," another broke in. "We have seen the sledges that your people use."

Caribou stared at them. "Can you, can you do this thing?" she whispered, then stopped herself, remembering the bridgeman, the hedgewives. "I have nothing to pay you with."

"You have already paid us," the fairest of the seamaidens said. She was the one who had taken Caribou's hand, and she wore a comb of red coral in her sea-green hair. She was holding a bundle in her arms. She offered it to Caribou now. "For you have given us hope, hope that the firelords may someday come to us, if only we can learn to love."

Caribou frowned, looking at the bundle the seamaiden held.

"Dress, dress," another standing beside the first urged then, and Caribou realized that what the other held out to her was her *lanlan* and other clothes, those she had discarded on the way down into the Fireking's realm.

"We gathered them up for you, that you might lose no time."

Numbly, she put on her clothes again, smock and leggings and outer boots, cap and *lanlan* and mitts. She did not feel overburdened with heat now; the presence of the sea-maidens kept the air around her pleasantly cool.

"We will take you up another stair," they said, motioning her to follow, "so that you will not need to pass the gateman again."

Caribou stopped short. "The gateman," she murmured. She had forgotten all about him. "I promised to return and tell him what befell me in the Fireking's hall . . ."

"No fear," the sea-maid with the comb in her hair

replied, smiling, "we will tell him the ending of your tale. He has already fallen asleep again by this time, and if you went back the other way, you would only wake him. Come."

Caribou allowed herself to be led away from the hall's entrance then, toward one of the long side walls. Into the stone of this wall, she saw, had been chiseled a stair which the sea-maidens motioned her to climb. They themselves came behind her so the sea water they trailed would not make the steps slippery.

As they climbed, higher and higher, the stone of the hall seemed to change into the earth itself. Caribou knew that they had left the hall of the Fireking then, though looking back she could still see it, far below, growing smaller.

The stair curved around and joined another, and Caribou guessed that the steps the sea-maidens had put her on must be the left-hand fork of the one she had taken down, the one the hedgewives had told her not to take. Caribou clenched her teeth.

"If I had taken this stair at the first," she exclaimed, "I would have come directly into the Fireking's hall, and avoided the gateman altogether."

The sea-maidens behind her said, "Yes, you should have come directly to us and not to those ugly troll-wives at all."

"They sent you down the other stair, most likely, because you beat them gambling. They hoped the bridgeman would not let you through. They do not like to lose."

Caribou felt a sudden twinge of apprehension. "But

what shall I do when I reach the top?" she asked. The hedgewives would be there. Already she could see daylight above. "I do not trust them now."

"All is well," the sea-maidens said. "We sang them to sleep while you were below. They will not stir again till spring."

Caribou's breath came easier then.

"Hurry," another maiden was saying now. "Already our sisters are singing back the sea."

"But how will I know when it is safe to begin to cross?" Caribou asked them, climbing, climbing the stair toward daylight and the upper air.

"Wait a little," they replied, "an hour or two — until the sun further declines and you begin to see the land. Then go."

"The sea will continue to fall," another maiden added, "until the sun is set and Greatmoon just barely risen. From then on the water will start to return, slowly."

"Do not delay, for you must be across by the time Greatmoon hangs at zenith in the sky and Littlemoon is just coming over the horizon's edge — for we cannot hold the sea back any longer than that."

The daylight was streaming into the tunnel now, nearly blinding her. Caribou blinked and climbed, feeling the crisp, cold sea air against her face.

"How will I know when we are safe?" she asked.

"You will have reached the landbridge's end, where it joins the snow-covered shore," the sea-maidens whispered. "You will have passed beside the Forge of the Fireking."

"Forge?" Caribou said. She had heard the word before, from Reindeer, once. "What is —?"

But the sea-maids were already shoving her through the tunnel's entrance, out into the world again.

"Haste, haste," they said. "Do not delay."

The sky above was very blue, the sun overhead just coming down from its height. Caribou tasted the sting of salt breeze on her lips. The circle of hedgewives all around was once more stone.

When she looked back over her shoulder, there were no sea-maids anymore in the tunnel's entrance, only puddles of sea water on the stairs, and here and there a draggle of kelp. Then the earth drew together again in a smooth, soundless snap like the closing of a drawstring bag, and Caribou stood alone.

17

The Song of
the Sea-Maidens

WHEN CARIBOU EMERGED from the trolls' hedge, she saw that the sea had grown shallower. The sandbar seemed wider now, with more of its surface exposed. She walked along it, back toward the crowd of sledges and people on the beach.

As she neared, she sensed an odd commotion, and realized that none of the people had taken any note of her. They all faced inward, toward her *gristal* not far from shore. Frowning, Caribou hurried closer — then saw with a start what had drawn her people's eyes.

Reindeer stood before her sledge, his head up, his eyes very wide and golden, as if daring any of her people to approach it. The breath from his nostrils made little spurts of steam. He pawed the shingle of the beach.

Tor stood facing him, as far away from the golden stag as he could get without stepping into the sea. From the tracks in the sand, Caribou could see how Reindeer had driven him away from her sledge, away from the others. The gold stag dodged, feinting at Tor, but the Tjaalsénji youth had stopped running.

He stood watching the *trangl*. His back was straight,

his face very pale, and though he had no weapon and nothing at hand that he might use for one, he did not look as if he meant to run from the golden daimon again. Tor cried out to him, "Why do you come at me and try to do me harm when I have done you no offense that I can see?"

Reindeer stamped and wheeled. Tor tensed, but held his ground. The gray waves licked at his heels.

"If you mean to drive me from your *gristal,* very well, I will not go there again — but I have ridden with you at the *i'dris*'s bidding, not on my own."

Caribou saw Reindeer give a great snort at the mention of her and come toward the tall youth suddenly, so that Tor fell back a pace. The sea-water splashed beneath his step. She hastened toward them along the beach.

The people stood silent, motionless, as if watching some storyteller. Their eyes were all fixed on Tor and Reindeer; no one seemed aware of her. Tor called out to the golden stag, "Why do you hesitate? You are a *trangl,* and I am unarmed. The *i'dris* has given me her protection — though I do not claim to deserve it — but I can see her wishes mean little to you when she is not here. Is she not your mistress, or is it you who . . . ?"

Without warning, Reindeer dropped his head and rushed at Tor. The young man had not yet finished speaking. There was nowhere for him to run. Caribou dashed along the beach and sprang between him and the charging stag. Flinging her arms out to keep Tor behind, she shouted, "Stop!" and heard people in the crowd cry out, dismayed.

Reindeer pulled up as quickly as he could, shying sharply away, but even so, one tine of his golden horns grazed her breast, tearing the soft leather of her *lanlan*. Caribou stared at him, more surprised than she had ever been, for her *trangl* had never offered her any harm in all his life. And though she knew those hooves, those horns had been meant for Tor, not for her, still she stared.

She could sense the young man standing motionless behind her. His breathing was shallow, and she could feel him shaking. She was shaking as well. She came away from him a few steps, her eyes on Reindeer.

"What are you doing?" she cried. "Why have you fallen on one of my people?"

Reindeer dropped his head a little, then raised it suddenly. She could not tell what he meant by that, only that he no longer seemed ready to spring at Tor. She kept herself between the two of them.

"*I'dris.*" It was Tor's voice behind her. She only half turned, afraid to take her eyes for long from Reindeer. Tor had knelt down at the water's edge. He seemed very weary suddenly. "*I'dris, my companions tried to steal from your gristal.*"

He pointed, and the crowd that still stood silent, transfixed, now drew back a bit. Caribou was hardly aware of them, only of Reindeer and Tor. For the first time she saw the two figures sprawled on the sand beside the sledge. One lay with her golden arrow in his hand. She was too astonished at first to speak.

"What happened?" she managed.

"I went . . . back to my companions," Tor told her. His voice was tight. "To see if I might sledge with them again."

"I told you not to do that," Caribou cried. Tor nodded.

"I know. But I did not wish to burden you anymore."

"You are no burden."

He had stopped then, looking at Reindeer. He spoke more softly. "And I know your *trangl* does not like me."

Reindeer snorted and stamped, so that Caribou glared at him.

"But my companions said — they said they would not take me back unless I helped them steal your golden arrow."

Caribou wheeled on Tor. She felt a hot flush of anger flooding her, and saw surprise mirrored in his eyes.

"Val had it in his head that this was the source of your magic, your dreams," he told her quickly. "He said if he could steal it, he could command your golden *trangl* and lead the people instead of you."

"Your companions are idiots," Caribou snapped. "I have always dreamed my dreams, and the only magic in that golden arrow is that it points toward where the reindeer are."

The crowd murmured then, protesting her words. Still they stood watching. Reindeer stamped.

"What happened then?" said Caribou to Tor. "What did you say to your companions?"

"I told them they were mad," exclaimed Tor, as if suddenly uncertain whether she believed him. "I said I would not help them."

Reindeer cavaled, pawing the sand.

"And then?"

"They shoved me aside and started for your sledge. I shouted at them to stop; I ran after — I shouted for others to help me stop them. But Orin already had the arrow in his hand."

"Why did none of you stop them?" Caribou demanded of the people around her. "Would you let two young thieves pillage your own sledges so?"

The crowd shifted and murmured. "We were afraid, *i'dris*," one woman said.

"Of them?" cried Caribou, with a glance at the fallen pair. She saw people shaking their heads.

"Of the arrow, *i'dris*," a man replied.

Caribou let out her breath. "It is only an arrow," she told them, "made golden by a *trangl*'s blood."

But the people cast down their eyes and would not look at her. Where were the councillors, Caribou wondered. She could not find Djenret or Brikka among the crowd. Were they hiding from her gaze? She clenched her teeth. Tor continued.

"When your *trangl* saw them, he rushed forward, and Val cried, 'You see! We have only to touch the arrow and he comes.' Orin held up the arrow before him and commanded, 'Halt,' as though certain your *trangl* would obey. But . . . your *trangl* . . ."

Tor paused there, fighting for breath.

". . . smote him down with his hooves," he said at last. "And when Val tried to flee, he tossed him with his horns. They lay still then — neither of them has moved since. They are dead. I am sure of it."

Caribou looked at the two lying on the strand. "But why did my *trangl* then come after you?" she said softly. "I thought you said you were not with them."

Tor shook his head. "I was not. I tried to go to them. I bent to take the arrow from Orin's hand."

"That was not wise," said Caribou.

"I meant no harm," cried Tor. "I meant only to put it back upon your sledge. I did not like to leave him holding it. But your *trangl* . . ."

"Yes," said Caribou. "Yes, I see. Go do it now. Go take the arrow from your companion's hand and stow it in my sledge."

The young man rose, then hesitated, eyeing Reindeer. Caribou said, not looking at him, still watching the golden stag, "Go on. My *trangl* will not harm you or any of my people ever again for no cause. I promise you that."

Tor went. Caribou listened to his footfalls crunching away across the shingle. She walked toward Reindeer, but he backed away from her, then wheeled and trotted. She followed, not running. They were half a hundred paces down the strand when at last he stopped and let her draw alongside him. And Caribou, who had never struck Reindeer a blow in all her life, felt very near doing so now.

"Why have you done that?" she hissed. "What is

the matter with you? Is this why you would not come with me when I asked, but left me to do it all alone — because you had another thing in mind to do while I was gone?"

Reindeer gazed down on her, motionless. She stood near enough to feel his breath. Her eyes narrowed.

"You may be able to guile others — even Tor, perhaps — into thinking you meant to kill him for touching some talisman of mine, but it is only an arrow, which you know as well as I. I have not weighed the hearts of men and sat in judgment, offering counsel, for as many years as you have been alive that you might guile *me* so. By the *waijen!* If I did not know you for a daimon that has no human heart, I would believe you are jealous of that boy because he has sledged with me."

Reindeer shook himself, very hard, and turned away from her — but Caribou grasped his antler in one hand so that he turned again, not because she had the strength to compel him, but from surprise. She had never touched him in anger before. Her breast ached where the tine of his horn had bruised her. She let go of his antler and took his head in her hands.

"What manner of daimon are you," she whispered, "that you can feel such a thing — regarding a stranger I have known only a handful of days? Do you not know, can you not see with your great gold eyes that seem to take in everything and tell me nothing, that it is only you I love — that I have loved you all your life?"

Her voice broke.

"Would you murder a boy, for nothing? Are you so treacherous — like the hedgewives, like the gateman of the Fireking? Can I not trust you? You promised that you would lead my people, *all* my people, safe into your winter land. And have I not said that I will come away with you, as soon as that is done?"

Reindeer stopped his snorting. The little spurts of steam from his nostrils grew calmer and less fierce. The pulse in his throat that had been beating wildly against her hand was quieting now. He touched his great, square nose to her breast and knelt down on the beach.

Caribou, kneeling as well, put her arms about his neck. He lay down and she leaned against him, stroking her fingers through his dense golden fur. She was so weary she could not stand. She wanted Reindeer in his man-shape again, if only for a moment, for an hour. She felt lost and desperate, for the sound of his voice, for the touch of his hand. But it was only a great golden stag that she held.

After a time, she rose and went back to tell her people what had befallen her in the trolls' hedge, and in the Fireking's realm below. While they waited for the sun to fall, she instructed them to see to their caribou, feed them lightly and check their hooves.

"Tend to your *gristaal* as well," she bade them. "Inspect the runners and see that your provisions are securely lashed down. Then tend to yourselves. Let all eat enough to sustain them, for we may be sledging half the night or more, and hard going."

She sought out Tor and spoke with him concerning his companions. They had neither fuel nor time to burn them properly, so she helped the young man scoop out a shallow trench for them on the beach and sing the dirge. Caribou wondered what tales their *waijen* would tell the bridgeman next spring when he raised the bridge and they crossed over into the Land of Everlasting Night. She and Tor covered them over with sand.

"I will take my companions' *gristal*," he told her then, "and not trouble you further."

Caribou rose, brushing the wet black grit from her hands and leggings. She eyed the young man a moment. His face was drawn but determined. Caribou nodded.

"Very well," she said. "I will give you half of what I carry." He made to protest, but she told him, "Peace. I brought enough, three times enough to keep me, and your sledge must have some weight, or it will run too light."

She and Tor unpacked her *gristal*, moving furs and foodstuffs to the hold of his, and lashing them down. As they worked, he told her a little of his life as it had been in Tjaalsénji. He was the son of a merchant, he said. Others, seeing how the *i'dris* favored the youth, seemed more kindly disposed toward him now, and gave him a little of their own *pisjlak* as well.

Caribou in turn told Tor of living alone, far from any town, on the edges of the Wilderland, offering judgments and counsel to people who came. She had never spoken of such to anyone before, not even Reindeer. Doing so now made her feel strangely bashful. She found herself blushing. The boy from Tjaalsénji had a beautiful, shy smile.

Reindeer watched the pair of them in silence from a little way down the beach. When at last the sun was languishing low in the sky, Caribou rose and went to him, put her arms around him and led him back to the sledge. As she buckled on the chinkling bells, she saw others around her putting up the last of their cooking pots, securing the lashings, and hurrying their draft-caribou into the traces.

Tor stood well away from Reindeer and a little behind Caribou as she regarded the sea. It had fallen at last. The shore before them stretched a long way into the sun-glared distance, and the water lay shallower off to either side. Caribou turned and walked back along the landboat toward the driver's step.

"*I'dris,*" said Tor, "the sun will be down in another hour, and Greatmoon will not rise till an hour after that. How will we see to follow you? How will you see the way?"

Caribou took her oil-pot from the sledge. She opened it. "That, too, I have dreamed," she said, and found herself able to smile again now, just a trace — for the reindeer's teeth upon her breast at last were whispering to her the meaning of one of her most troubling dreams.

She walked with the pot back toward Reindeer. Tor followed, careful still to remain well back — but the *trangl* hardly gave him a glance.

"The landbridge is narrow," Caribou told Tor. "So

the others cannot go far wrong. There will be moonlight, and the sound of my *trangl*'s bells."

She grasped Reindeer's harness then and shook it. The bells tinkled like crystal ice.

"Still . . ." the youth replied.

Caribou nodded, smiling. "I know." She put her hand into the pot until her fingers were covered with the soft, slurry stuff — it did not solidify, even in the cold. Then she smeared the yellow oil along the tips of Reindeer's horns. He bowed his head that she might reach them, ignoring Tor.

The Tjaalsénji youth stood watching her, no less baffled, while Caribou scrubbed her hand clean with some of the black grit from the beach. Then she fetched her golden arrow from the sledge and dipped the point of it into the oil. She closed the pot and stored it. Tor continued to watch her.

"*I'dris* . . ." he said.

Caribou handed him the arrow. He started violently as she pressed it into his hand. He glanced at Reindeer, but the *trangl* stood gazing off. Caribou kept her hand on Tor's a moment to steady him.

"Go to Brikka," she said, "that woman there who has not yet covered her fire. Light the tip of this arrow, and bring it back to me. Then we will go."

Caribou went and took the driver's step while Tor did as she had told him. He brought the golden arrow with its burning point back to her, and she tied it to the railing with a thong, the burning tip upright and well away from the wood of the sledge.

The fire on the arrow had almost no color, seemed

only a rippling in the air about the arrow's head and a thread of smoke. The young man watched her a moment more, then went to take his place on the step of his own *gristal*. Caribou turned to her waiting people.

"We must be off," she cried, "for the sea-maidens have sung the waves back from the land, and we must pass while we may."

"But *i'dris*," someone cried, "how shall we see you in the dark?"

"You will see me," answered Caribou. "Have no fear."

"But wisewoman," another man called, "how long will the landbridge last?"

"The water will fall," answered Caribou, "until Greatmoon begins to rise. The sea will then be at its lowest point. From moonrise on, the waves will begin to return — slowly. So let us make what speed we can."

She clapped the reins and Reindeer sprang away. With a shout, the others in their *gristaal* followed. The seadogs that had lounged upon the dry land in their path fled before them, humping away across the shallows toward the retreating waves. The landbridge lay before them like the backbone of the sea.

The sun fell down the western sky like a great, burning bird. At last it rolled gently into the sea, dousing itself amid clouds of low-lying steam. Caribou listened for the hiss, or for some hint of the sea-maidens' song, but she could hear nothing above the plangent surf and the singing of Reindeer's bells.

Night fell. Shade by shade the sky darkened. The stars overhead reflected in the waves, so that the land-bridge seemed surrounded by stars. At last Caribou took the burning arrow from the rail. The tip blazed in the blackness now with a brilliant, white-yellow light that hardly seemed to flicker.

Far ahead of the others, she pulled Reindeer to a halt and darted forward along the sledge's length, then sprang from the landboat's toe onto Reindeer's back. He stood still without flinching, steady as a house as Caribou touched the flaring arrow to his oil-smeared horns.

They caught, all the tips in a wreath of light, blazed up in a white glow that danced like summer light-ning — it hardly seemed to be flame at all. She heard Tor, heard others behind her crying out in surprise.

Caribou leapt lightly back to the sledge and back to the driver's box. The other *gristaal* had almost drawn even with her now. Still holding the golden arrow, she gathered the reins in her other hand. Reindeer sprang, and they were off again, into the utter black-ness of the night.

The fierce red glow in the west that had been the sunset gradually faded. The stars seemed very many and far away, while the flame in Caribou's hand and upon Reindeer's horns barely guttered in the chill, evening wind. Their brightness lit the dark.

The shingle beach was slick and smooth, the going swift. The sea continued to retreat, exposing more and more of the black beachhead. Greatmoon rose, a ghostly face, pale and glaring, silver-white.

The tide was at its lowest ebb. The moon floated above the flat rim of the world beside them, scarcely an arm's reach away, it seemed. The landbridge spread before them, black and gleaming.

The polar cluster of stars burned like a fistful of jewels directly overhead, and the only sound in the stillness was the gusting of the cold, light sea-breeze, the crash and wash of distant breakers, and the high, clear singing of the bells.

They sledded for hours over the left-hand bank. The firth had now opened out into a vast bay that stretched to their right. By moonlight, she could barely spot the other side. As they sped, Caribou saw sea-beasts that leapt in graceful arcs, frolicking in the shallow sea.

Square, flat animals with many legs — hard-bodied like spiders — danced sideways under the moonlight in the shallow tide-pools. A flock of great birds, larger than fish hawks, skimmed barely a hand's breadth above the combers with the moon in their wings. The ice-mountains, like crystal houses, drifted serenely along the horizon's edge, back-lighted by the low, rising moon.

As Greatmoon began to rise higher, the beach beneath their runners became more slick, the sea water slowly welling up. It seeped through the cinder-like sand — only a few fingers deep at first, then in little running ripples that swept from the eastern sea toward the firth.

"Haste!" Caribou cried, above the jangled burring of the bells. "We must make haste. The sea returns!"

How long this spine of black cinders would continue she did not know. The sea-maidens had given them only a handful of hours. She wondered how long it took the reindeer to cross. *We are slower than they.* She knew — all her people knew — if they had not reached higher ground by the time Greatmoon had reached its zenith and Littlemoon was just beginning to rise, they were lost.

She felt Reindeer's pace becoming swifter. The bells chanted more loudly, in quicker rhythm. She held the burning arrow high, heard the others clapping their reins and tapping their willows across the backs of their teams. The beach beneath their runners sloshed and ground, awash with shallow waves, as Greatmoon slowly mounted the dark blue, star-pitted sky.

18

The Forge of
the Fireking

THE SMOOTHNESS of the fine-grained cinders beneath the runners began to change. The surface
grew rocky, seamed and slippery, still of that same
black stone. The right-hand bank of the firth had long
since fallen away, and a single high peak rose against
the stars in the distance before them.

Caribou peered, trying to make out the shadowy
peak beyond the flare of Reindeer's burning. The peak
seemed oddly conical, like a potter's kiln, plunging
steeply away into the sea on either side. It spanned
the whole width of the landbridge they traveled.

Caribou's heart contracted violently — they would
never get their sledges over those plunging slopes
. . . ! And then she made out faintly, by moonlight,
a long line of shallow breakers foaming landward,
never quite reaching the cliffs: a narrow beachhead
allowing passage around the mountain on one side.

But the tightness beneath her breastbone did not
ease. How long would it take them to reach the strand?
The night was so dark; she could not judge. How
long to skirt the mountain, and how far beyond it lay
the landbridge's end? Greatmoon was more than half-

way to its zenith: the draft-caribou were in water midway to their knees, and the broad sledge-runners were nearly submerged beneath the shallow waves.

If the water rises much further, she realized, *if we do not reach the mountain soon, there will be no beachhead at all to cross, leaving us trapped between that black peak and the sea.* Caribou shoved the thought away. She dared not clap the reins to Reindeer. If he ran any swifter, he would outdistance the others.

They came at last to a place where the land began to rise, and Caribou heard her people shouting with relief. The water around them fell away by degrees. The closer to the dark mountain they drew, the higher and drier the ground beneath their *gristal*-runners became.

But Caribou could not join in her people's rejoicing, for the surface of the beach was hilly and pitted here, no longer smooth, as though the earth had been much disturbed. Great rills extended from the mountain's foot like long toes into the sea, their ups and downs impeding the progress of the gristaal.

Glancing back, Caribou glimpsed drivers and passengers leaping down now and again to help shoulder their sledges along. Some of the troughs between the rills went down very deep. Her golden *trangl* avoided these, and the echoes thrown back from their darkness had an eerie sound.

Taps and groans and sometimes creakings came to her ears — like the blows of smiths' hammers or the workings of a great bellows. What had Reindeer told her once, about the firelords' mining of the earth? *Are they below us now,* she wondered, *forging their precious silver and their gold?*

The speculation alarmed her somehow. She tried to shut her mind, but the image persisted, vivid and bright, of the firelords with their beards of fire, shaping the burning metal with hammer and tongs.

The teeth upon her breast chattered and clicked, unintelligibly. The bells of Reindeer's harness ranted and chimed. Caribou flinched as sometimes a fierce heat drafted up from the troughs, as though their depths plumbed for leagues, straight down into the fiery heart of the world.

Their *gristaal* had reached the slopes of the mountain now and were skirting along toward the low, curving beach. A mere ribbon of sand still showed between the cliffs and the incoming waves. All at once, Caribou noticed a dull glow shining between cracks in the mountainside, a reddish light that grew brighter and stronger with each crevice they passed.

Others among the band had seen it as well. She listened to their cries of bewilderment, wonder, alarm. Then someone called out something new, his voice harsh with surprise. Other voices caught up the cry. Caribou cast about her, trying to see what they saw. She spotted Tor on the driver's step of his *gristal,* only a few paces behind her. He raised one arm toward the summit overhead.

"*I'dris,* look!"

Caribou stared. As they rounded one bend of the conical slope, shoving over the last of the long fingers down to the beachhead below, she saw that the peak above had fallen away, like the rim of a broken bowl. Through the gap, she beheld a sea of glowing stone.

Smoking, it churned, the steam roiling dull red into a black, starry sky. Within the crater, little fountains spewed like spurting stars. Littlemoon, a wan blue eye, was just peering over the rim of the sea to the east of them. Greatmoon hung suspended at its zenith above.

The mount erupted with a roar. It started as a trembling in the earth, then thundered suddenly to a rumbling shout, like a geyser bursting. Bits of fire, like flocks of birds, leapt into the dark night-sky, and the white moon overhead turned coppery, like blood.

The caribou brayed and bolted then. Caribou saw one *gristal* overturned and dragged into the sea. She shouted, tried to call out to her people, but the mountain's blast carried her words away. Reindeer gave out a belling cry. Caribou heard it clearly through the haze of other noise, the mountain's thunder and her people's screams.

The caribou quieted at the sound, slowing their frenzied flight. She saw one group with an overturned sledge manage to right it again. The earth trembled, but less violently now. Fire continued to spew from the mouth of the mount, but none of it was falling far enough downslope to reach them.

Caribou signaled with her burning arrow for her people to hasten, to guide their *gristaal* after her along the black ribbon of beach. Reindeer's horns were a white wreath of fire. He called again to the teams, and they followed him. Gazing up, Caribou saw liquid firestone spilling over the crater's rim like spattered broth.

Glowing, feverish red, the fiery river crept down the mountain's slope. Caribou felt a sickening jolt — *if it reaches the beach before we do, if it flows across and blocks our path, we will be trapped, cut off from the white snowy plains just coming into view ahead, drowned in the rising waves.*

Caribou slapped the reins and called. Reindeer quickened his pace effortlessly. They flew over the smooth, wet, black beachhead. The incoming tide had made it so narrow in places that two sledges could scarcely run abreast. Caribou and her people made their way halfway around the mountain's side, and then further, nearly three-quarters of the way.

The tremors and deafening rumbles of the mountain grew more violent. Fountains of brimstone spouted into the sky. Smoking ash and cinders began to fall. She heard screams of caribou and people touched by the particles. She glimpsed Tor behind her, crouching and holding a skin over his head. Caribou ducked down as far as she could into her *lanlan,* smelling the stench of scorched leather and hair.

The fireflood crept down the mountainside like the bright blood of the earth. It loomed just ahead; it had nearly reached the strand. The air above it shivered and burned. Caribou cried out to her people: words, anything. She pointed forward with her arrow at the fields of snow beyond.

They were on the beach. All around her, teams of

caribou shied and balked. Caribou pulled back, trying to slow Reindeer. She would not leave her people, and she would not let them stop. Using her willow switch, she hied the balking teams. Shouting, she dragged them by the bit. Reindeer belled out his golden cry, and the caribou came on.

The heat grew fierce, gusting and billowing. All Caribou could see was red. She felt flushed, drenched in her heavy *lanlan,* and clawed at its latches to open the throat. Her knees weakened. She felt herself fainting against the rail.

Then, all at once, they were past. The slowly advancing river of firestone fell behind. A blast of frigid air brought her awake again, invaded her *lanlan,* chilled her to the bone. She latched the throat closed again. Turning, she watched the other sledges behind her coming, and felt a stab of fear until she saw Tor's among them, passing the narrow point and flying out onto the wide, open beach beyond.

The last ones got by. Their caribou were staggering. Caribou saw passengers and several drivers swooned upon their sledges, but the caribou ran on, following Reindeer's cry. Further back, well behind the last *gristal,* with a howling hiss and towering plumes of steam, the fireflood merged into the sea.

The broad cinder beach ground flat and loose beneath her sledge's runners now. Another half mile and they would reach the snow. She looked back just once more before they came upon that white expanse.

Beneath the red violence of the flaring mountain, in a recess on the southwestern face of the peak, near

its foot, all seemed quiet — strangely so. In the recess
lay a pool, where a fountain gushed, its color visible
even in the pale leaching light of Greatmoon: pure
gold.

As golden as her *trangl's* coat, his golden eyes, his
spattered blood — as golden as Reindeer's hair in his
man-shape, that fountain rose. Caribou felt her sledge
leap up behind Reindeer onto the deep-packed snow.
Still looking back, wonderstruck, she kept her eyes
on the Forge of the Fireking, beside which stood
spouting the Fount of Gold.

Their sledges sped over the plain of snow, deep
clean white snow that showed the passage of a vast
herd of deer before them. They followed the wide cut
of that passage, fleeing the burning mountain and the
Firth of Fire.

And after the moons set on them that night, very
low in the north, they never rose again, nor did their
companion the sun, until Caribou and her people had
neared their journey's end, though they traveled many
sleeps over the Country of Unbroken Snow.

The people were much afraid, fearing that they had
passed into the Land of Everlasting Night, for often,
directly above them as they camped, the ghostly *waijen* danced, long shimmering ribbons of blue, violet,
and green.

But Caribou spoke words of comfort to her folk
beside their fires, telling old tales to ease their minds
and new tales, to give them heart, of the land beyond.

They followed her grimly, without complaint. They had no choice, she realized. They could not go back.

At last they left the Plain of Endless Snow, and the *waijen*'s dance fell away in the darkness behind. The sun rose again, hanging low and bright in the sky, and the moons as well. Once again they had the day to travel by and the night for sleep. Reindeer's horns and Caribou's arrow finally burned themselves out.

Caribou and her people found themselves passing over tundra again, as flat and featureless as the frozen plains they had known in the country they had left behind. In a few days' time, the tundra gave way to hills, and trees covered with late-autumn snow.

Eventually they passed down out of the high country, into sheltered valleys of dry, yellow grass, where snow had not yet fallen. Wearily, Caribou led them past the first such valley, and the second as well.

Her people were angry then, crying out that they longed to rest, to settle and build their winter shelters. But Caribou refused to call a permanent halt, insisting, "We have not yet found the place that I have spoken of, the place that is to be our home."

"How is it we will know it, *i'dris?*" Djenret asked her.

But Caribou, her brow wrinkled with determination, would only say, "I will know it, and so will you."

They drove on, until they had passed into the third valley. At last Caribou called a halt. She was utterly spent. She ached from all the days they had sledged and all the nights she had spent sleepless, reassuring her disspirited followers, from all the cold and hardship. But she was smiling now.

"Here we will settle," she declared.

A moment of startled silence, then a ragged cheer rose from the sledges behind.

"But why here?" asked Brikka softly, her *gristal* drawn alongside Caribou's. "*I'dris,* how is this valley different from the others we passed through?"

With her arrow, Caribou pointed down the slope toward the meadow below them. "What do you see there?" she asked.

The councilwoman looked, staring at the gray specks dotting the sides of the far-off meadow. The air was crisp and clear.

"The wild deer!" Caribou heard Tor's voice behind her exclaim.

She only laughed and shook her head. "Not the wild deer," she answered, clapping the reins to Reindeer to bear her downslope toward the meadow. "Our caribou."

19

Strangers

IT WAS SIX WEEKS still to the solstice when they reached their journey's end, and the first snows long overdue. Caribou felt a sense of wonder. Was it only a month they had traveled in their sledges — four short littlemoons? She had lost all sense of time in the sunless Region of Endless Snow. It had seemed much longer. She was weary to the bone.

Jubilation overshadowed her weariness though, as she watched her people settle into the broad, protected valley, building hasty enclosures for their caribou and felling trees to make shelters for themselves before snowfall. The weather continued sunny and mild.

Nuts, fish, wild fruits and game were all abundant. Families began laying in their stores. There were daimons in every tree and rock, it seemed, accepting the offerings left for them. The little charms people said — against ill-luck or to help untangle a cord or plane a board — began to work again, and there was magic once more in the shamans' talismans and bones.

Caribou's people had been in their new land scarcely two littlemoons when the elders of the council called for a feast in honor of Caribou. Bonfires were set in the sandy clearing between the two streams wending through the vale, and there was much carousing and toasting of the *i'dris* with draughts of herbal tea and berry cider.

Both moons were full and high in the sky. Tor sang his silly song about the end of the world and the falling sky till the company roared, stamping in time. Then all of them tossed their guest of honor in a blanket, higher and higher, until Caribou thought she might touch the moons. They shouted, *"I'dris! I'dris!"* tossing, until Caribou grew dizzy and made them stop. She had never laughed so hard in her life.

But when she staggered back to her sledge at last, long after midnight, Reindeer was not there. She had been so busy overseeing her people's settling in that she had not had time even to choose a place for building her own *ntula*. The aportioning of land was the council's job, but they could not do it all, and the people trusted Caribou's judgment. Besides, she enjoyed the work. It exhilarated her.

Reindeer had remained with her. By day he drifted through the trees, never far from her sight but unwilling to join her among her people. By night he lay beside the sledge where she slept — but always in deer-shape. He would not change. And Caribou, impatient, felt even more frustrated that she could not ask him why.

This was the first night he had ever left her alone. Caribou stood beside the sledge in the moonlight, vexed and bewildered. She called for him once, but got no answer. He did not come. Caribou undressed and climbed beneath the caribou skins on her sledge.

She was too muzzy-headed to go looking for him.

Perhaps it is just as well that he is not here and in his man-shape, she found herself thinking uncertainly as she drifted into sleep. *I have fallen asleep the moment I lay down every night since we came here.* She dreamed of Tor and the others toasting her, and not drawing away or making the sign against evil when she approached. She dreamed of touching the moons.

By morning Reindeer had not returned. Caribou awoke late, feeling strained and cross. Her joints were stiff. She dressed with a growing feeling of panic, casting about her through the trees, searching their brown and red and black for a glimpse of gold. *No more of this,* she told herself finally. *He cannot be far. He would not leave me.*

She did not go into the settlement that day. Instead, she climbed high up one rocky slope to a spot overlooking the vale. Her head still ached a little from the revel the night before. The morning light made her wince. From below, the sound of ax and mallet rang out sharply in the crisp, cool air, and the shouts of workers calling to one another. She thought she might even have caught a faint snatch of Tor's song, from far away, sung by someone else.

Below, most of the half-finished houses clustered along the streams, but others were scattered here and there about the slopes. She stood higher than them all. Soon, she knew, there would not be one family or group that had sledged together that did not have at least a low roof over their heads.

Except for me, thought Caribou, and sighed. *I have been minding my people's lives so long I have forgotten my own. Dying-summer will not last forever. I must set to work. I have delayed too long.*

"Is this the spot where we shall build your *ntula?*" a voice behind her asked.

Caribou spun around. She had not heard that voice since they had left the Wilderland, forever ago, on the other side of the world. Reindeer in his man-shape was coming toward her out of the trees. With a cry of joy, she ran to him.

"I thought you would never come away from the others," he said. His face had no expression. His eyes were just the same. She clung to him, laughing, all her aches vanished. He put his arms around her and kissed her, and she knew then, beyond all doubt, that he had longed for her these past weeks as urgently as she had longed for him.

"Stay now," she told him. "Stay in your man-shape with me."

He pulled her down to the grassy ground with him. "I will stay in my man-shape all winter with you."

Reindeer and Caribou built their *ntula,* felling trees, raising the roof and caulking the walls. After the building, there was much to be done in the way of gathering, preserving, and storing. Caribou's provisions were nearly exhausted. She went down daily into the settlement to arbitrate disputes and advise the council. No one came to her *ntula* to trouble her and Reindeer.

At last the snows of winter came. With their *gristaal,* Caribou's people ranged far afield in search of stores: wood, game, fodder for their caribou. They saw no sign of other people, no track or trap, no house or smoke, tamed beast or bird. The land seemed completely virgin, untrespassed by any — until a few days before solstice, when Djenret and Brikka sought Caribou out in her hut.

"*I'dris,*" they told her, "we have seen strangers. They have come to us in the village below, two of them, a boy and a woman, driving a sledge drawn by a troika of strange beasts."

Caribou served her guests flat cakes of acorn meal and elder tea upon the doorstep of her hut. She spotted Tor among the little group that had come with the two elders. Seeing him, she felt an unexpected twinge, part plain happiness at seeing him and finding him well, part an odd uneasiness in his presence. Behind her, Reindeer lingered in his man-shape within the darkness of the hut, reluctant to show himself, she knew, but listening.

"These deer —" the youth from Tjaalsénji was telling her. The two elders stepped back, acknowledging the special place that he held with their wisewoman. "These deer that draw the strangers' sledge," he said, "they are larger than our caribou, rounder of body and coarser of head. I saw them close. Their hooves are not divided, but solid, a single toe."

Caribou sat listening, trying not to smile. The young man's face was alive, his fascination clear. He gestured as he spoke.

"They have long tails, too, of silky hair, and a fringe of the same running along their necks. Little ears, no horns — like calves. But they wear bridles and tack, and seem as docile as caribou."

"Tell me of the strangers themselves," murmured Caribou, sipping her tea.

"They are odd." Brikka spoke now. "Their garments are of woven cloth, in bright colors, like the River-Valley Folk. Their hair is brown, but of a lighter color than our hair. The boy's has a red cast to it. Their skin is not olive like ours, but the color of cream. The woman's eyes are brown — but again, a lighter brown. The boy's eyes are oddly pale, as gray as glass."

Caribou ground the dense, coarse acorn cake between her teeth and thought a moment, not smiling now. Tor was watching her from the group. His gaze upon her made her restless.

"You have greeted them?" she asked.

The others nodded.

"Made them welcome?"

"Aye."

Caribou set down her cup, fingered the golden arrow on her lap. Across from her, Djenret of Vlad stood tugging on his moustache.

"We want you to come look at them, *i'dris,*" he told her. "Talk to them and discover what they want."

Caribou scratched her arm, eyeing the councillor. Intrigued as she was by the news of these strangers, her people's expectation puzzled her. She had led them safe into a new land, as she had promised, but she was not their chieftain. They had no chieftain. The council ruled.

"These strangers," she inquired, "do they refuse to talk to the council?"

Brikka came forward now. "They are ready and willing to talk to the council, *i'dris*. We want them to talk to you."

Caribou frowned, keenly aware now for the first time how much the elders relied on her in making their decisions. She thought of Reindeer suddenly, in the dark of her hut, listening. *I must not let them become too dependent on me,* she thought suddenly, worried, *for I will not be here after the spring.* A few paces away she saw Tor studying her. She turned back to the councilman again.

"Djenret," she exclaimed, "you head the council of elders. I am only a wisewoman —"

Tor's words cut her off. "You are our *i'dris!*" He stopped, disconcerted at his own outburst, but recovered quickly. "You led us across the Land of Everlasting Night. Of course we have come to you." His voice had a different timbre from Reindeer's: darker, full of emotion. He came forward and knelt before Caribou. "Please come, *i'dris*," he said.

His perfect seriousness — as if he truly thought she did not mean to come — made Caribou laugh. Rising, she took his empty cup from him, and those from the others standing before her. "Very well," she told them. "I will come."

Going back into the hut, she laid the teacups by the firepit and spoke to Reindeer, sitting far from the coals' heat and light. The beauty of his goldenness seemed diminished somehow, lost in shadow. She went to him.

"I am going down into the valley to see these strangers," she said. "Will you come with me?"

He shook his head.

"Not even in deer-shape?"

Again he shook his head.

"What is it?" she asked, drawing near. "You seem . . . melancholy." She had to search for the word. She had never thought to use such a word for him. He looked at her then, with that fathomless expression that had come to seem almost a smile — gone rueful now?

"I am a *trangl,*" he told her, removing his hand gently from hers, "and *traangol* can be neither melancholy nor glad."

She eyed him for a long moment, but could not read him. She almost wished that she might stay then, or that he would come, but she had no time to coax him further. Tor and the others waited. Reluctantly, she rose.

"I will tell you of these strangers when I return."

Caribou went with the townspeople down the steep, rocky slope to see the two strangers in the village below. She spotted them, the woman and the boy, beside their *gristal* drawn by the peculiar, undeerlike deer, in the sandy clearing between the two streams.

"Greetings, strangers; our guests, and be welcome," Caribou said, as was fitting, while the council members stood looking on from a few paces back, and other townsfolk clustered about the clearing's edge. "I am Caribou, whom my people call their *i'dris*. Tell me your names, if you will, and why you have come."

The woman stepped forward, all grace and self-possession. She was older than Caribou, and she wore ornaments of carved amber, like a shaman.

"Greetings, seer," she said, smiling. "I am called Olwen. I, too, am priestess to my people, who live north of here. This is Sigl" — she gestured to the boy — "my son and acolyte. We came to gather gold-berry for our celebration of the winter solstice, before the hard snows come and cut us off from here. But from afar we saw the smoke of your fires. We did not know that any tribe lived here. We have always called these the Unclaimed Lands."

Caribou smiled a little then, to herself, and gestured around her at the rude hovels surrounding the square. "As you see, Olwen, we are but lately arrived and newly settled. Great upheavals in the earth of our homeland drove us away. We sought new country to settle in."

Watching Olwen's cream-colored face, Caribou saw surprise there, but the priestess's manner remained gracious.

"Where do you come from?" Olwen asked.

Caribou forgave the baldness of it. Perhaps, like the River-Valley People, Olwen's tribe did not consider such questions forward. Caribou gestured.

"We come from there, beyond the Pole. Over the Burning Plain and the Cinderlands we came, passing beside the Firth of Fire, over the Backbone of the Sea, beside the Forge of the Fireking, and over the Plain of Unbroken Snow, where neither moon nor sun ever shine. We sledged, following the wild deer from the other side of the world."

Caribou saw growing astonishment in Olwen's face, in the boy's, open-mouthed awe that was almost fear. He stared at Caribou.

"From the other side of the world?" whispered Olwen. "From beyond the Pole? Then you are . . . you are from the Golden Lands."

She seemed at a loss for the first time, and sought Caribou's eyes, as if to reassure herself that the other truly stood there.

"Our legends tell of a people who dwell there," Olwen breathed. "And just this autumn past, a year ago, two of my acolytes met in these hills a golden man who said he had come from there . . ."

Caribou remembered Reindeer telling her how he had learned the workings of a *gristal* by helping two children repair theirs. She smiled and nodded. "He brought word of your country back to us and led us here. But we have never called the lands where we used to dwell golden —"

Just at that moment, one of the village sledges pulled into the clearing. Caribou realized in surprise that it was Tor upon the driver's step — when had he slipped away? A great pile of branches laden with yellow waxbud lay lashed on the prow.

At the sight of the sledge, Olwen cried out, "Oh,

surely you must be they — for your *gristaal* are drawn by the great deer, tame as any horses or kine!"

Tor guided his team near, reined to a halt, and leapt down. He lifted a bundle of branches from the hold.

"*I'dris,*" he said, "I heard these strangers say they had come searching for goldberry, but I saw none in their sledge. I went to cut some."

Caribou nodded and answered, "You did well."

He handed a bundle to the acolyte. The gray-eyed boy took the branches reverently, staring at Tor as if the young man might suddenly change into a bird before his eyes.

Olwen turned back to Caribou with a similar look, and seemed about to speak, when across the stream appeared the village's caribou, driven by young children on foot with long willow switches. They were bringing the herd down from the high pastures, for the sun had already fallen low enough to shade the best slopes.

Some of the caribou bent to drink, and the children halted, gazing at the crowd across the stream. Djenret started to shoo them away, but Caribou took his arm and said, "Let them be."

Olwen had ceased staring. She folded her wrists across her breast and made a deep obeisance to Caribou.

"Surely you are they, the divine ones from the Golden Lands, great *i'dris,*" she murmured. "You have clothed yourselves in mortal shape, but who could fail to recognize you? For the wild deer run meekly before the swats of your children."

Caribou shook her head and knelt down beside Olwen.

"These are not the wild deer," she answered, "but caribou, their tame cousins. The wild deer have run on before us to their wintering grounds north of here."

"Oh, yes," Olwen replied, her head still bowed, not looking at Caribou. "They winter on the verges of our country, and roam wherever they will. We do not molest them, for they belong to you. The herd-beasts of the gods are sacred to us."

Caribou laid her hand upon the other woman's arm.

"Olwen," she said, "my people are no gods — not even little ones — but flesh. We are a Tribe, villagers and woodfolk, like you."

The strange priestess raised her eyes slowly. At last she uncrossed her hands. Her face was very pale, her skin like ice, but Caribou's touch seemed to reassure her. When Caribou rose, Olwen rose with her.

"You have said so much, and I have seen such things," she said uncertainly, "that my head aches with it. I must think on all of this."

She glanced toward her son. Caribou saw that Tor and the boy had loaded all of the waxbud into the strangers' *gristal*.

"Sigl and I must start homeward now," Olwen said, "or we will not reach our village before the heavy snows." She glanced at Caribou again, still half in puzzlement and half in awe.

"Will you come again," said Caribou, "in spring, Olwen, when the rains have gone? Then the leaders

of your people and our leaders, the council, may con-
fer."

She felt oddly uneasy as she said that — not at
the thought of Olwen or her people, but because
she was speaking of her Tribe's future, which she
would not be present to share. She thought of
her promise to Reindeer and felt a stab of bitter
regret.

She would miss her people, very sorely. They had
accepted her, and she had learned to live among them
at last. Angrily, she shoved regret away. Her promise
to the *trangl* had saved all their lives. *And I love him.
I need him. I want to be with him. I have given my word;
now I must be content.*

With an effort, Caribou turned her thoughts
back to Olwen. What had they just spoken of? Oh
yes, of the leaders of Olwen's people coming in
the spring. The pale-skinned woman nodded to
Caribou. She seemed uncertain, but determined
to act.

She shooed her son up into the sledge before her.
Caribou saw with fascination that it was driven from
a bench mounted high in the forepart, not at the
rear, as with their own *gristaal*. The boy sat on the
bench.

Olwen turned and bowed to Caribou before climbing to take her place beside the boy. Caribou, unsure
whether the priestess's gesture had been meant simply
as a politeness upon parting or as a reverence, carefully
returned it.

The priestess caught up the reins of her strange,

long-faced beasts and whistled to them, turning them, and glided out of the settlement, away over the hilly terrain. Caribou watched with the others until the sledge was lost among the trees on the northern slope, then turned to go back to her hut.

20

The People of Caribou

WHEN SHE REACHED HOME, Caribou told Reindeer of the meeting, of the strangers' words, of their new kind of *gristal,* and of their promise to come again in springtime with their chieftains — but all the while she spoke, her golden youth remained pensive and silent.

"I know what is troubling you," she told him at last. "You are weary of your man-shape and restless to run with the reindeer again. Why do you not go?"

She spoke quietly, touching his arm, but her teeth were clenched. She had to force herself to say the words — not because she wanted him to leave her, but because she knew she had no power to hold him if he wished to be gone.

"My hut here is built and my stores all laid in. I would not starve to death or freeze this winter, if you were to go away."

Evening outside was dark, and within the hut only firelight illuminated him. As she spoke, she felt him shiver. He turned to her quickly, taking her hands, and gazed at her very intently.

"No, Cari," he whispered. "I will stay with you.

The reindeer will not die of longing for me, either, if I stay away a little more."

She leaned against him then, so glad she could scarcely speak, and felt his strong arms about her. "Stay with me till springtime," she said. "My people will be settled by then, and have no more need of me."

No more need of me. She willed away the sudden sharp ache that the thought caused her. She willed it to be the truth. He stroked her hair.

"Then when the reindeer run southward again," he murmured, "back to the other side of the world where your people used to dwell, you will go with me as you promised, and bathe in the Fount of Gold."

Reindeer stayed with her that winter, casting off his deer-shape all through the months of snow. Caribou tried to be happy, to think only of the present. She did not want to think about the spring. She clung to him almost desperately now and could hardly bear to be parted from him, but he seemed to have no wish to be anywhere but at her side.

It troubled her, though, that they were not undisturbed. Despite the distance and the hard climb to her hovel, people from the settlement below often made the steep journey to receive her judgment or ask for advice. Though she knew she ought not to encourage them — for she would not be among them much longer — Caribou could not turn any of them away.

Reindeer always sat within when her people came, listening from the darkness of the hut and not emerging until they had gone, even if the consultation took

all morning or all afternoon. Or else he went away
into the woods when he saw them climbing toward
the house — returning only after sunset at the end of
the day.

The best days were the ones they spent alone together, when no one came. Then Caribou could forget
her people, forget all obligations to any but herself,
and think only of Reindeer. Even so, her golden youth
was often silent.

When she tried to discover why, he answered none
of her gentle questions, or answered distantly. More
than once, he was gone from the hut when she awoke
at dawn, staying away long hours, and would say
nothing of where he had been. Her dreams did not
help her understand him. They never had.

Spring came. The snow upon the slopes grew soft,
trickling down to swell the streams. Caribou had hoped
that the return of warmth and sun would lighten her
golden *trangl's* mood, but Reindeer only seemed to
become more troubled.

She felt his restlessness, and the golden arrow's
twitch, and knew the reindeer would be running soon.
The prospect filled her with dread. Soon Reindeer
would hold her to her promise. Putting on his deer-
shape again, he would carry her away.

She tried to resign herself to it, to feel glad. The
running of the wild deer would mean that she might
leave behind this life with all its mortal cares, and
these people, from whom she had always felt so different.

But I am not an outcast anymore! she found herself

thinking desperately one night. *I want to stay here with my people. They need me. We are just beginning here.* And yet she loved Reindeer with all her heart and did not know how she could live without him. She felt as if she were being torn in two.

Then one day when Reindeer was away, the sixteen elders made the difficult climb to her hovel. Tor came with them, and the elders all stood back to let the young man speak. He made their supplication eloquently, speaking of the people's great love for her.

Caribou felt cold with surprise. Her belly clenched. She answered very shortly and sent the astonished councillors away. Tor stayed behind, without her bidding, but she refused to meet his concerned, inquiring eyes.

"*I'dris,* what is it?" he asked at last. "Surely you knew we would ask you this?"

She sat on the threshold of her hut, half turned away from him. She shook her head. "My mind has been on other things this winter past," she said. "I did not guess."

"Have we angered you?" His words were soft.

She almost laughed — not from mirth. She felt like weeping instead. "The council *honors* me," she whispered.

He came and knelt beside her. "But you are sad, *i'dris.* Why?"

She turned to look at him. "I owe a debt," she said, "a debt to my *trangl.*" She had not meant to speak of it, but now that she had started, she found she could not stop. "In exchange for his leading us safe to this new land, I have promised to go away with him."

She saw the young man's eyes widen. "Go?" he whispered. "Go where, when?"

"*Now,* soon, when the reindeer are running." She was angry at Tor suddenly for no reason. The golden arrow twitched in her hand. She had begun to shake. Then she blurted out, "I do not want to go."

She felt a sudden pressure on her wrist. Tor had reached to take hold of it. "*I'dris,* don't," he said. "Don't go with him." She shook her head and tried to pull away, but Tor held on. "Tell him you wish to stay with us," the young man said urgently. "He will release you. If he loves you, he must."

And she remembered how she had said almost the same thing once, to Branja, a very long time ago. She stopped struggling and gazed at Tor's very young and human face. She realized whom he reminded her of suddenly: of Visjna, her brother. She put her fingers to the spot on his cheek where the gray water had burned him. The skin was pale there still. Of Reindeer, she said:

"But you speak as though he were a man. He is not a man. Did you think the *traangol* do anything for love?" *Even though* I *love* him, she added silently. To Tor she said, "And I have given him my word."

He seemed to realize only then that he had taken hold of her. He dropped her wrist. She saw him blushing. Caribou drew away from him and rose.

"Go back to the village," she told him. "I must treat with my *trangl* now."

"*I'dris,*" he began, his dark eyes beseeching her, but she shook her head.

"Go," she told him gently. "These things are between my *trangl* and me."

Tor did not rise at first, but she turned away and after a little she heard him go. After he had gone, she went inside the hut. She felt as though she were dying inside. Her abdomen knotted and cramped. A great weight oppressed her heart. She sat by the firepit till evening and wept.

Reindeer came into the hut. His figure blocked the twilight in the doorway. He threw off his reindeer cape, which he wore fur-side in so that the skin of the pelt would not cleave to him and make him a reindeer. He stood pinning shut the flap of stitched hide that was their door; then turning, he seemed to see for the first time that she was weeping. He came to her, and knelt.

"Why are you doing that?" he said, touching her cheek.

Caribou brushed at the tears impatiently. "Where did you go?" she cried. "Where were you all day — why weren't you here?"

"What has happened?" he asked.

"The elders came."

"What of them?"

Caribou's throat was too tight to speak. She swallowed. "They have chosen a new chieftain for the Tribe."

"You weep for that?"

She looked at him, into his changeless, fathomless golden eyes that she could never understand. "They have chosen *me*."

He showed no surprise. "But you told them no."

She looked away. "I . . . told them I would think on it." She felt fresh tears hot upon her cheeks. Reindeer, she knew, was still watching her.

"Why did you not tell them you were going away?"

Caribou bit her lip. "I don't know. I don't know." Her voice was a whisper. She had told Tor — but he was not a member of the council.

A little silence then.

"You promised to come away with me in the spring."

She shut her eyes, shook her head, put both hands to her face. Her belly felt like a wound that had healed drawn and sore. She bent over. "I know that," she whispered. "I know."

She felt the young man's hard arms fold about her then, drawing her up. She put her own arms about his neck and pressed her face to his shoulder, but holding him was no comfort to her.

"How can I leave now?" she gasped. "My people need me. The chieftains of the milk-skinned strangers will be coming, and who will treat with them if I am gone? Then the planting must be begun — the villagers have asked me to allot the land for their fields. They trust me. They want me to stay."

She struggled and could hardly find the words.

"The People of Caribou. That is what they are calling themselves now — did you know it? And they make no distinction between the term we call our herdbeasts and the word which is my name. How may I go with you now? How may I go? It isn't finished yet, what I have begun."

His face never changed, but she felt a tremor pass through his arms. She had never seen him flinch before. Suddenly, she could not look at him. Her voice deserted her. And Reindeer held her still, gently, almost absently, his gaze expressionless.

When at last her weeping ceased, he said, "Tomorrow, go down to the settlement and call your sixteen elders to you. Tell them that you accept their offer. Tell them you will be their chief."

The words startled her. She tried to pull away, but the band of his arms neither tightened nor yielded.

"But . . ." She shook her head. "I promised you."

His voice grew even softer then, as though something stopped his throat. He could only breathe, "I forgive you your promise to me."

She felt something burning splash down the side of her face, and then another drop of fire upon her neck. She leaned back a little, saw Reindeer touch each of his eyes, bewildered, and stand staring at the golden liquid on his fingertips.

"Are these tears?" he said. "I have never wept before."

She touched the gold on his cheeks. It burned her fingers, hot as tallow. He looked up at the touch.

"You used to tell me, Cari, that I had no human heart. But I think that it has become human — or more human — now, because of you. Or perhaps it was only that that side of me deeply slept, and you have wakened it, for knowing that I must run with the wild deer without you a while is making a great pain in my breast."

She wiped the gold tears from his cheeks. She remembered the strange, hot dart she had felt the very first time she had taken him into her house, and on the night of his return from the wild deer. She said to him, "You have the power to compel me to come."

His breath caught strangely. He answered, "No. I will not bind you. I do not wish to take from you what is not freely offered." He touched his breast. "I do not want you to feel this pain that I am feeling now. And I know that you will feel it if you come with me before you have finished here."

He shook his head, as if to clear it, with a kind of grimace — and then she saw that he was trying to smile. It came easier on the second try. The unearthly fair features of his face became near-human suddenly. He looked almost mortal then. She had never seen him more beautiful. He cradled her face between his hands.

"But I will come to you each autumn and spring, to ask you if you are finished yet."

He turned and went to the little chest where she kept his things — man-clothes and boots, traces and bells, and the gifts she had once carved him from the golden stag's bones. Reindeer lifted the lid and took out the long haft of reindeer horn — the only piece Caribou had never finished. He returned with it to the firepit, held out the haft to her.

"I have known since autumn," he sighed, "that you

would not come with me. All winter I have been making this."

Taking it, she saw that it was wondrously carved, beyond all human skill, with tiny figures that told the story of his life and Caribou's: how Branja had brought to her the babe; how his father had stolen him away and then fallen beneath her brother's arrow; how he himself had gone away to join the wild deer — and then returned to help Caribou lead her people beyond the Burning Plain. The lower end of the haft was left uncarved.

"What is it?" she asked softly.

"A chieftain's wand. Your people brought none of the old one's things with them when they came away." Caribou knelt, holding the bone wand in both her hands. "The other half," he said, "is for you to carve. Show it to me when I come to you every winter and spring, and I will see if you have finished it."

Reindeer rose, pulling off his man-clothes and laying them aside.

"Keep these for me," he said, "till I return. And promise me —" He touched her belly lightly with one hand. She looked at him, but did not draw away. "I promise you that I will not bear our child away, as my father tried to do with me."

His golden eyes looked into hers.

"But promise me in return that you will send our son to me when he is old enough."

She stared at him, and felt cold with wonder suddenly, though the room was warm. "How did you know?" she whispered. "I was not even sure myself. I did not want to tell you until I was sure."

He looked at her. His golden eyes lightened. "I am a *trangl*," he said, kissing her. "We always know."

She felt her breath catch in her throat, and clung to him. All at once she felt light: no sorrow anymore. It was as if a great stone had been lifted from her. She wanted to laugh, and found she was weeping again. He took her hands in his.

"One day," he said, looking deep into her with his golden eyes. "One day you will come with me."

He stood away from her and turned, reaching to catch up the golden pelt.

"Wait," she cried. "Wait." She could not bear to let him go. "I trust you," she found herself saying, "and know that you will keep your word to me concerning our child — but how if others of your kind come among my people again, to charm them, and lie with them, and steal their children?"

Reindeer turned to her. "Once I had hoped you would come among us and bring the *traangol* to your understanding. But since you cannot come with me yet, it is I who must speak to my people now, and dissuade them."

"Will they listen?" she asked.

He pressed her hands. "They will listen. They must — I will tell them the People of Caribou forbid such things. And if any *trangl* shall come among your people," he said, "and seek to charm them against their will, I will put a stop to it."

She touched his cheek — but he pulled free of her and stepped away. He threw his golden pelt around him, skin-side to his skin. Caribou fell back, but did not hide her eyes from the change, as she always had before.

What she saw was a golden light leaping from the pelt to edge Reindeer round in a sharp line, like the sun behind a cloud. Then, instantly, his form collapsed from that of a man into that of an antlered stag. The light faded. Caribou stood dazzled.

She heard a rush and the clatter of hooves, felt a moment's cold air. Silence then. Presently, she heard one of the great deer belling, off down the slope across the valley somewhere, and the thunder of many heels. She stood, still starstruck, the drum of running reindeer filling the night. Her senses returned only gradually. The chieftain's wand in her hand felt heavy and cool.

When at last she could see again, she was aware of the dim glow of the firepit behind her, the hut door unpinned and flapping in the gaunt night breeze, and beyond that, by moonlight, far away, the wild deer streaming through the valley below. Southward, Poleward, they ran. Her golden Reindeer was with them.